W9-BYK-823

Numbers Don't Lie

Selected Books by Terry Bisson

FICTION

Wryldmaker (1981)
Talking Man (1986)
Fire on the Mountain (1988)
Voyage to the Red Planet (1993)
Bears Discover Fire and Other Stories (1996)
Pirates of the Universe (1996)
In the Upper Room and Other Likely Stories (2000)
The Pickup Artist (2001)
Greetings (Tachyon, 2005)

MEDIA TIE-INS

Johnny Mnemonic (1995)
The Fifth Element (1997)
Alien Resurrection (1997)
Galaxy Quest (1999)
The X Files: Miracle Man (2000)
Boba Fett: Crossfire (2003)

NONFICTION

Nat Turner: Slave Revolt Leader (1988)
On a Move: The Story of Mumia Abu Jamal (2001)
Tradin' Paint: Raceway Rookies and Royalty (2001)

COLLABORATIONS

Saint Leibowitz and the Wild Horse Woman with Walter Miller, Jr. (1997)
Car Talk with Click and Clack, the Tappet Brothers with Tom and Ray
    Magliozzi (1991)

TERRY BISSON
Numbers Don't Lie

TACHYON PUBLICATIONS | SAN FRANCISCO

Numbers Don't Lie
Copyright © 2005 by Terry Bisson

Cover illustration by Cory & Catska Ench
Cover design © 2005 by Ann Monn.
Interior design & composition by John D. Berry.
The typeface is Dolly.

Tachyon Publications
1459 18th Street #139
San Francisco, CA 94107
(415) 285-5615
www.tachyonpublications.com

Series Editor: Jacob Weisman

ISBN: 1-892391-32-5

Printed in the United States of America
by the Maple-Vail Book Manufacturing Group

First Edition: 2005

9 8 7 6 5 4 3 2 1

"The Hole in the Hole" copyright © 1994 by Bantam Doubleday Dell Magazines. First published in *Asimov's Science Fiction Magazine*, February 1994.

"The Edge of the Universe" copyright © 1996 by Bantam Doubleday Dell Magazines. First published in *Asimov's Science Fiction Magazine*, August 1996.

"Get Me to the Church on Time" copyright © 1998 by Bantam Doubleday Dell Magazines. First published in *Asimov's Science Fiction Magazine*, May 1998.

Previously published in e-book format by ElectricStory: ISBN B00005BBB2 (2001)

Sson.
Terry

Contents

To my reviewers:

Smart, good-looking, and generous, every one.

Numbers Don't Lie

The Hole in the Hole

TRYING TO FIND Volvo parts can be a pain, particularly if you are a cheapskate, like me. I needed the hardware that keeps the brake pads from squealing, but I kept letting it go, knowing it wouldn't be easy to find. The brakes worked okay — good enough for Brooklyn. And I was pretty busy, anyway, being in the middle of a divorce, the most difficult I have ever handled, my own.

After the squeal developed into a steady scream (we're talking about the brakes here, not the divorce, which was silent), I tried the two auto supply houses I usually dealt with, but had no luck. The counterman at Aberth's just gave me a blank look. At Park Slope Foreign Auto, I heard those dread words, "dealer item." Breaking (no pun intended) with my usual policy, I went to the Volvo dealer in Bay Ridge, and the parts man, one of those Jamaicans who seems to think being rude is the same thing as being funny, fished around in his bins and placed a pile of pins, clips, and springs on the counter.

"That'll be twenty-eight dollars, mon," he said, with what they used to call a shit-eating grin. When I complained (or as we lawyers like to say, objected), he pointed at the spring which was spray-painted yellow, and said, "Well, you see, they're gold, mon!" Then he spun on one heel to enjoy the laughs of his coworkers, and I left. There is a limit.

So I let the brakes squeal for another week. They got worse and worse. Ambulances were pulling over to let me by, thinking I had priority. Then I tried spraying the pads with WD-40.

Don't ever try that.

On Friday morning I went back to Park Slope Foreign Auto and pleaded (another legal specialty) for help. Vinnie, the boss's son, told me to try Boulevard Imports in Howard Beach, out where Queens and Brooklyn come together at the edge of Jamaica Bay. Since I didn't have court that day, I decided to give it a try.

The brakes howled all the way. I found Boulevard Imports on Rockaway Boulevard just off the Belt Parkway. It was a dark, grungy, impressive-looking cave of a joint, with guys in coveralls lounging around drinking coffee and waiting on deliveries. I was hopeful.

The counterman, another Vinnie, listened to my tale of woe before dashing my hopes with the dread words, "dealer item." Then the guy in line behind me, still another Vinnie (everyone wore their names over their pockets) said, "Send him to Frankie in the Hole."

The Vinnie behind the counter shook his head, saying, "He'd never find it."

I turned to the other Vinnie and asked, "Frankie in the Hole?"

"Frankie runs a little junkyard," he said. "Volvos only. You know the Hole?"

"Can't say as I do."

"I'm not surprised. Here's what you do. Listen carefully because it's not so easy to find these days, and I'm only going to tell you once."

There's no way I could describe or even remember everything this Vinnie told me: Suffice it to say that it had to do with crossing over Rockaway Boulevard, then back under the Belt Parkway, forking onto a service road, making a U-turn onto Conduit but staying in the center lane, cutting a sharp left into a dead end (that really wasn't), and following a dirt track down a steep bank through a grove of trees and brush.

I did as I was told, and found myself in a sort of sunken neighborhood, on a wide dirt street running between decrepit houses set at odd angles on weed-grown lots. It looked like one of those leftover neighborhoods in the meadowlands of Jersey, or down South, where I did my basic training. There were no sidewalks but plenty of potholes, abandoned gardens, and vacant lots. The streets were half-covered by huge puddles. The houses were of concrete block, or tarpaper, or board and batten; no two alike or even remotely similar. There was even a house trailer, illegal in New York City (so, of course, is crime). There were no street signs, so I couldn't tell if I was in Brooklyn or Queens, or on the dotted line between the two.

The other Vinnie (or third, if you are counting) had told me to follow my nose until I found a small junkyard, which I proceeded to do. Mine was the only car on the street. Weaving around the puddles (or cruising through them like a motorboat) gave driving an almost nautical air of adventure. There was no shortage of junk in the Hole, including a subway car someone was living in, and a crane that had lost its verticality and took up two backyards. Another backyard held a piebald pony. The few people I saw were white. A fat woman in a short dress sat on a high step talking on a portable phone. A gang of kids was gathered around a puddle killing something with sticks. In the yard behind them was a card table with a crude sign reading MOON ROCKS Я US.

I liked the peaceful scene in the Hole. And driving through

the puddles quieted my brakes. I saw plenty of junk cars, but they came in ones or twos, in the yards and on the street, and none of them were Volvos (no surprise).

After I passed the piebald pony twice, I realized I was going in circles. Then I noticed a chain-link fence with reeds woven into it. And I had a feeling.

I stopped. The fence was just too high to look over, but I could see between the reeds. I was right. It was a junkyard that had been "ladybirded."

The lot hidden by the fence was filled with cars, squeezed together tightly, side by side and end to end. All from Sweden. All immortal and all dead. All indestructible, and all destroyed. All Volvos.

The first thing you learn in law school is when not to look like a lawyer. I left my tie and jacket in the car, pulled on my coveralls, and followed the fence around to a gate. On the gate was a picture of a snarling dog. The picture was (it turned out) all the dog there was, but it was enough. It slowed you down; made you think.

The gate was unlocked. I opened it enough to slip through. I was in a narrow driveway, the only open space in the junkyard. The rest was packed so tightly with Volvos that there was barely room to squeeze between them. They were lined up in rows, some facing north and some south (or was it east and west?) so that it looked like a traffic jam in Hell. The gridlock of the dead.

At the end of the driveway, there was a ramshackle garage

made of corrugated iron, shingleboard, plywood, and fiber-glass. In and around it, too skinny to cast shade, were several ailanthus — New York's parking-lot tree. There were no signs but none were needed. This had to be Frankie's.

Only one living car was in the junkyard. It stood at the end of the driveway, by the garage, with its hood raised, as if it were trying to speak but had forgotten what it wanted to say. It was a 164, Volvo's unusual straight six. The body was battered, with bondo under the taillights and doors where rust had been filled in. It had cheap imitation racing wheels and a chrome racing stripe along the bottom of the doors. Two men were leaning over, peering into the engine compartment.

I walked up and watched, unwelcomed but not (I suspected) unnoticed. An older white man in coveralls bent over the engine while a black man in a business suit looked on and kibitzed in a rough but friendly way. I noticed because this was the late 1980s and the relations between black and white weren't all that friendly in New York.

And here we were in Howard Beach. Or at least in a Hole in Howard Beach.

"If you weren't so damn cheap, you'd get a Weber and throw these SUs away," the old man said.

"If I wasn't so damn cheap, you'd never see my ass," the black man said. He had a West Indian accent.

"I find you a good car and you turn it into a piece of island junk."

"You sell me a piece of trash and..."

And so forth. But all very friendly. I stood waiting patiently until the old man raised his head and lifted his eyeglasses, wiped along the two sides of his grease-smeared nose, and then pretended to notice me for the first time.

"You Frankie?" I asked.

"Nope."

"This is Frankie's, though?"

"Could be." Junkyard men like the conditional.

So do lawyers. "I was wondering if it might be possible to find some brake parts for a 145, a 1970. Station wagon."

"What you're looking for is an antique dealer," the West Indian said.

The old man laughed; they both laughed. I didn't.

"Brake hardware," I said. "The clips and pins and stuff."

"Hard to find," the old man said. "That kind of stuff is very expensive these days."

The second thing you learn in law school is when to walk away. I was almost at the end of the drive when the old man reached through the window of the 164 and blew the horn: two shorts and a long.

At the far end of the yard, by the fence, a head popped up. I thought I was seeing a cartoon, because the eyes were too large for the head, and the head was too large for the body.

"Yeah, Unc?"

"Frankie, I'm sending a lawyer fellow back there. Show him that 145 we pulled the wheels off of last week."

"I'll take a look," I said. "But what makes you think I'm an attorney?"

"The tassels," the old man said, looking down at my loafers. He stuck his head back under the hood of the 164 to let me know I was dismissed.

Frankie's hair was almost white, and so thin it floated off the top of his head. His eyes were bright blue-green, and slightly bugged out, giving him an astonished look. He wore cowboy boots with the heels rolled over so far that he walked on their sides and left scrollwork for tracks. Like the old man, he was wearing blue gabardine pants and a lighter blue work shirt. On the back it said —

But I didn't notice what it said. I wasn't paying attention. I had never seen so many Volvos in one place before. There was every make and model — station wagons, sedans, fastbacks, 544s and 122s, DLS and GLS, 140s to 740s, even a 940 — in every state of dissolution, destruction, decay, desolation, degradation, decrepitude, and disrepair. It was beautiful. The Volvos were jammed so close together that I had to edge sideways between them.

We made our way around the far corner of the garage, where I saw a huge jumbled pile — not a stack — of tires against the fence. It was cooler here. The ailanthus trees were waving, though I could feel no breeze.

"This what you're looking for?" Frankie stopped by a 145 sedan — dark green, like my station wagon; it was a popular color. The wheels were gone and it sat on the ground. By each wheel well lay a hubcap, filled with water.

There was a hollow thud behind us. A tire had come over

the fence, onto the pile; another followed it. "I need to get back to work," Frankie said. "You can find what you need, right?"

He left me with the 145, called out to someone over the fence, then started pulling tires off the pile and rolling them through a low door into a shed built onto the side of the garage. The shed was only about five feet high. The door was half-covered by a plastic shower curtain hung sideways. It was slit like a hula skirt and every time a tire went through it, it went *pop*.

Every time Frankie rolled a tire through the door, another sailed over the fence onto the pile behind him. It seemed like the labors of Sisyphus.

Well, I had my own work. Carefully, I drained the water out of the first hubcap. There lay the precious springs and clips I sought — rusty, but usable. I worked my way around the car (a job in itself, as it was jammed so closely with the others). There was a hubcap where each wheel had been. I drained them all and collected the treasure in one hubcap. It was like panning for gold.

There was a cool breeze and a funny smell. Behind me I heard a steady *pop, pop, pop*. But when I finished and took the brake parts to Frankie, the pile of tires was still the same size. Frankie was on top of it, leaning on the fence, talking with an Indian man in a Goodyear shirt.

The Indian (who must have been standing on a truck on the other side of the fence) saw me and ducked. I had scared him away. I realized I was witnessing some kind of illegal dumping operation. I wondered how all the junk tires fit into the tiny shed, but I wasn't about to ask. Probably Frankie and the old man took them out and dumped them into Jamaica Bay at night.

I showed Frankie the brake parts. "I figure they're worth a couple of bucks," I said.

"Show Unc," he said. "He'll tell you what they're worth."

I'll bet, I thought. Carrying my precious hubcap of brake hardware, like a waiter with a dish, I started back toward the driveway. Behind me I heard a steady *pop*, *pop*, *pop* as Frankie went back to work. I must have been following a different route between the cars—because when I saw it, I knew it was for the first time.

The 1800 is Volvo's legendary (well, sort of) sports car from the early 1960s. The first model, the P1800, was assembled in Scotland and England (unusual, to say the least, for a Swedish car). This one, the only one I had ever seen in a junkyard, still had its fins and appeared to have all its glass. It was dark blue. I edged up to it, afraid that if I startled it, it might disappear. But it was real. It was wheelless, engineless, and rusted out in the rocker panels. But it was real. I looked inside. I tapped on the glass. I opened the door.

The interior was the wrong color—but it was real, too. It smelled musty, but it was intact. Or close enough. I arrived at the driveway, so excited that I didn't even flinch when the old man looked into my hubcap (like a fortune-teller reading entrails) and said, "Ten dollars."

I raced home to tell Wu what I had found.

*

Everybody should have a friend like Wilson Wu, just to keep them guessing. Wu worked his way through high school as a pastry chef, then dropped out to form a rock band, then won a scholarship to Princeton (I think) for math (I think), then dropped out to get a job as an engineer, then made it halfway through medical school at night before becoming a lawyer, which is where I met him. He passed his bar exam on the first try. Somewhere along the line he decided he was gay, then decided he wasn't (I don't know what his wife thought of all this); he has been both democrat and republican, Catholic and Protestant, pro and anti gun-control. He can't decide if he's Chinese or American, or both. The only constant thing in his life is the Volvo. Wu has never owned another kind of car. He kept a 1984 240DL station wagon for the wife and kids. He kept his P1800, which I had helped him tow from Pennsylvania, where he had bought it at a yard sale for five hundred dollars (a whole other story), in my garage. I didn't charge him rent. It was a red 1961 sports coupe with a B18. The engine and transmission were good (well, fair) but the interior had been gutted. Wu had found seats but hadn't yet put them in. He was waiting for the knobs and trim and door panels, the little stuff that is hardest to find, especially for a P1800. He had been looking for two years.

Wu lived on my block in Brooklyn, which was strictly a coincidence as I knew him from Legal Aid, where we had both worked before going into private practice. I found him in his kitchen, helping his wife make a wedding cake. She's a caterer. "What are you doing in the morning?" I asked, but I didn't wait for him to tell me. I have never been good at surprises (which is why I had no success as a criminal lawyer). "Your long travail is over," I said. "I found an 1800. A P1800. With an interior."

"Handles?"

"Handles."

"Panels?"

"Panels."

"Knobs?" Wu had stopped stirring. I had his attention.

"I hear you got your brakes fixed," Wu said the next day as we were on our way to Howard Beach in my car. "Or perhaps I should say, 'I don't hear.'"

"I found the parts yesterday and put them on this morning," I told him. I told him the story of how I found the Hole. I told him about the junkyard of Volvos. I told him about stumbling across the dark blue P1800. By then, we were past the end of Atlantic Avenue, near Howard Beach. I turned off onto Conduit and tried to retrace my turns of the day before, but with no luck. Nothing looked familiar.

Wu started to look skeptical; or maybe I should say, he started to look even more skeptical. "Maybe it was all a dream," he said, either taunting me or comforting himself, or both.

"I don't see P1800s in junkyards, even in dreams," I said. But in spite of my best efforts to find the Hole, I was going in circles. Finally, I gave up and went to Boulevard Imports. The place was almost empty. I didn't recognize the counterman. His shirt said he was a Sal.

"Vinnie's off," he said. "It's Saturday."

"Then maybe you can help me. I'm trying to find a place called Frankie's. In the Hole."

People sometimes use the expression "blank look" loosely. Sal's was the genuine article.

"A Volvo junkyard?" I said. "A pony or so?"

Blank got even blanker. Wu had come in behind me, and I didn't have to turn around to know he was looking skeptical.

"I don't know about any Volvos, but did somebody mention a pony?" a voice said from in the back. An old man came forward. He must have been doing the books, since he was wearing a tie. "My Pop used to keep a pony in the Hole. We sold it when horseshoes got scarce during the War."

"Jeez, Vinnie, what war was this?" Sal asked. (So I had found another Vinnie!)

"How many have there been?" the old Vinnie asked. He turned to me. "Now, listen up, kid." (I couldn't help smiling; usually only judges call me "kid," and only in chambers.) "I can only tell you once, and I'm not sure I'll get it right."

The old Vinnie's instructions were completely different from the ones I had gotten from the Vinnie the day before. They involved a turn into an abandoned gas station on the Belt Parkway, a used car lot on Conduit, a McDonald's with a dumpster in the back, plus other flourishes that I have forgotten.

Suffice it to say that, twenty minutes later, after bouncing down a steep bank, Wu and I found ourselves cruising the wide mud streets of the Hole, looking for Frankie's. I could tell by Wu's silence that he was impressed. The Hole is pretty impressive if you are not expecting it, and who's expecting it? There was the non-vertical crane, the subway car (with smoke coming from its makeshift chimney), and the pony grazing in a lot between two shanties. I wondered if it was a descendant of the old Vinnie's father's pony. I couldn't tell if it was shod or not.

The fat lady was still on the phone. The kids must have heard us coming, because they were standing in front of the card table waving hand-lettered signs: MOON ROCKS THIS WAY! and MOON ROCKS Я US! When he saw them, Wu put his hand on my arm and said, "Pull over, Irv,"—his first words since we had descended into the Hole.

I pulled over and he got out. He fingered a couple of ashy-looking lumps, and handed the kids a dollar. They giggled and said they had no change.

Wu told them to keep it.

"I hope you don't behave like that at Frankie's," I said, when he got back into the car.

"Like what?"

"You're supposed to bargain, Wu. People expect it. Even kids. What do you want with phony moon rocks anyway?"

"Supporting free enterprise," he said. "Plus, I worked on Apollo and I handled some real moon rocks once. They looked just like these." He sniffed them. "Smelled just like these."

He tossed them out the window into the shallow water as we motored through a puddle.

As impressive as the Hole can be (first time), there is nothing more impressive than a junkyard of all Volvos. I couldn't wait to see Wu's face when he saw it. I wasn't disappointed. I heard him gasp as we slipped through the gate. He looked around, then looked at me and grinned. "Astonishing," he said. Even the inscrutable, skeptical Wu.

"Told you," I said. (I could hardly wait till he saw the 1800!)

The old man was at the end of the driveway, working on a diesel this time. Another customer, this one white, looked on and kibitzed. The old man seemed to sell entertainment as much as expertise. They were trying to get water out of the lines.

"I understand you have an 1800," Wu said. "They're hard to find."

I winced. Wu was no businessman. The old man straightened up, and looked us over. There's nothing like a six-foot Chinaman to get your attention, and Wu is six-two.

"P1800," the old man said. "Hard to find is hardly the word for it. I'd call it your rare luxury item. But I guess it won't cost you too much to have a look." He reached around the diesel's windshield and honked the horn. Two shorts and a long.

The oversized head with the oversized eyes appeared at the far end of the yard, by the fence.

"Two lawyers coming back," the old man called out. Then

he said to me, "It's easier to head straight back along the garage till you get to where Frankie is working. Then head to your right, and you'll find the P1800."

Frankie was still working on the endless pile (not a stack) of tires by the fence. Each one went through the low door of the shed with a *pop*.

I nodded, and Frankie nodded back. I turned right and edged between the cars toward the P1800, assuming Wu was right behind me. When I saw it, I was relieved — it had not been a dream after all! I expected an appreciative whistle (at the very least), but when I turned, I saw that I had lost Wu.

He was still back by the garage, looking through a stack (not a pile) of wheels against the wall.

"Hey, Wu!" I said, standing on the bumper of the P1800. "You can get wheels anywhere. Check out the interior on this baby!" Then, afraid I had sounded too enthusiastic, I added, "It's rough but it might almost do."

Wu didn't even bother to answer me. He pulled two wheels from the stack. They weren't exactly wheels, at least not the kind you mount tires on. They were more like wire mesh tires, with metal chevrons where the tread should have been.

Wu set them upright, side by side. He slapped one and gray dust flew. He slapped the other. "Where'd you get these?" he asked.

Frankie stopped working and lit a cigarette. "Off a dune buggy," he said.

By this time, I had joined them. "A Volvo dune buggy?"

"Not a Volvo," Frankie said. "An electric job. Can't sell you the wheels separately. They're a set."

"What about the dune buggy?" Wu asked. "Can I have a look at it?"

Frankie's eyes narrowed. "It's on the property. Hey, are you some kind of environment man or something?"

"The very opposite," said Wu. "I'm a lawyer. I just happen to dig dune buggies. Can I have a look at it? Good ones are hard to find."

I winced.

"I'll have to ask Unc," Frankie said.

"Wu," I said, as soon as Frankie had left to find his uncle, "there's something you need to know about junkyard men. If something is hard to find, you don't have to tell them. And what's this dune buggy business, anyway? I thought you wanted interior trim for your P1800."

"Forget the P1800, Irv," Wu said. "It's yours. I'm giving it to you."

"You're what?"

Wu slapped the wire mesh wheel again and sniffed the cloud of dust. "Do you realize what this is, Irv?"

"Some sort of wire wheel. So what?"

"I worked at Boeing in 1970," Wu said. "I helped build this baby, Irv. It's off the LRV."

"The LR what?"

Before Wu could answer, Frankie was back. "Well, you can look at it," Frankie said. "But you got to hold your breath. It's in the cave and there's no air in there."

"The cave?" I said. They both ignored me.

"You can see it from the door, but I'm not going back in there," said Frankie. "Unc won't let me. Have you got a jacket? It's cold."

"I'll be okay," Wu said.

"Suit yourself." Frankie tossed Wu a pair of plastic welding goggles. "Wear these. And remember, hold your breath."

It was clear at this point where the cave was. Frankie was pointing toward the low door into the shed, where he rolled the tires. Wu put on the goggles and ducked his head; as he went through the doorway he made that same weird *pop* the tires made.

I stood there with Frankie in the sunlight, holding the two wire mesh wheels, feeling like a fool.

There was another *pop* and Wu backed out through the shower curtain. When he turned around, he looked like he had seen a ghost. I don't know how else to describe it. Plus, he was shivering like crazy.

"Told you it was cold!" said Frankie. "And it's weird. There's no air in there, for one thing. If you want the dune buggy, you'll have to get it out of there yourself."

Wu gradually stopped shivering. As he did, a huge grin spread across his face. "It's weird, all right," he said. "Let me show my partner. Loan me some extra goggles."

"I'll take your word for it," I said.

"Irv, come on! Put these goggles on."

"No way!" I said. But I put them on. You always did what Wu said, sooner or later; he was that kind of guy.

"Don't hold your breath in. Let it all out, and then hold it. Come on. Follow me."

I breathed out and ducked down just in time; Wu grabbed my hand and pulled me through the shed door behind him. If I made a *pop* I didn't hear it. We were standing in the door of a cave — but looking out, not in. The inside was another outside!

It was like the beach, all gray sand (or dust) but with no water. I could see stars but it wasn't dark. The dust was greenish gray, like a courthouse hallway.

My ears were killing me. And it was cold!

We were at the top of a long, smooth slope, like a dune, which was littered with tires. At the bottom was a silver dune buggy with no front wheels, sitting nose down in the gray dust.

Wu pointed at it. He was grinning like a maniac. I had seen enough. Pulling my hand free, I stepped back through the shower curtain and gasped for air. This time I heard a *pop* as I went through.

The warm air felt great. My ears gradually quit ringing. Frankie was sitting on his tire pile, smoking a cigarette. "Where's your buddy? He can't stay in there."

Just then, Wu backed out through the curtain with a loud *pop*. "I'll take it," he said, as soon as he had filled his lungs with air. "I'll take it!"

I winced. Twice.

"I'll have to ask Unc," said Frankie.

*

"Wu," I said, as soon as Frankie had left to find his uncle, "let me tell you something about junkyard men. You can't say 'I'll take it, I'll take it' around them. You have to say, 'Maybe it might do, or...'"

"Irving!" Wu cut me off. His eyes were wild. (He hardly ever called me Irving.) He took both my hands in his, as if we were bride and groom, and began to walk me in a circle. His fingers were freezing. "Irving, do you know, do you realize, where we just were?"

"Some sort of cave? Haven't we played this game before?"

"The Moon! Irving, that was the surface of the Moon you just saw!"

"I admit it was weird," I said. "But the Moon is a million miles away. And it's up in the..."

"Quarter of a million," Wu said. "But I'll explain later."

Frankie was back, with his uncle. "That dune buggy's one of a kind," the old man said. "I couldn't take less than five hundred for it."

Wu said, "I'll take it!"

I winced.

"But you've got to get it out of the cave yourself," the old man said. "I don't want Frankie going in there anymore. That's why I told the kids, no more rocks."

"No problem," Wu said. "Are you open tomorrow?"

"Tomorrow's Sunday," said the old man.

"What about Monday?"

*

I followed Wu through the packed-together Volvos to the front gate. We were on the street before I realized he hadn't even bothered to look at the 1800. "You're the best thing that ever happened to those two," I said. I was a little pissed off. More than a little.

"There's no doubt about it," Wu said.

"Damn right there's no doubt about it!" I started my 145 and headed up the street, looking for an exit from the Hole. Any exit. "Five hundred dollars for a junk dune buggy?"

"No doubt about it at all. That was either the Hadley Apennines, or Descartes, or Taurus Littrow," Wu said. "I guess I could tell by looking at the serial numbers on the LRV."

"I never heard of a Hadley or a Descartes," I said, "but I know Ford never made a dune buggy." I found a dirt road that led up through a clump of trees. Through the branches I could see the full Moon, pale in the afternoon sky. "And there's the Moon, right there in the sky, where it's supposed to be."

"There's apparently more than one way to get to the Moon, Irving. Which they are using as a dump for old tires. We saw it with our own eyes!"

The dirt road gave out in a vacant lot on Conduit. I crossed a sidewalk, bounced down a curb, and edged into the traffic. Now that I was headed back toward Brooklyn, I could pay attention. "Wu," I said. "Just because you worked for NAPA—"

"NASA, Irv. And I didn't work for them, I worked for Boeing."

"Whatever. Science is not my thing. But I know for a fact that the Moon is in the sky. We were in a hole in the ground, although it was weird, I admit."

"A hole with stars?" Wu said. "With no air? Get logical, Irv." He found an envelope in my glove compartment and began scrawling on it with a pencil. "No, I suspected it when I saw those tires. They are from the Lunar Roving Vehicle, better known as the LRV or the lunar rover. Only three were built and all three were left on the Moon. Apollo 15, 16, and 17. Nineteen seventy-one. Nineteen seventy-two. Surely you remember."

"Sure," I said. The third thing you learn in law school is never to admit you don't remember something. "So how did this loonie rover get to Brooklyn?"

"That's what I'm trying to figure out," Wu said. "I suspect we're dealing with one of the rarest occurrences in the Universe. A neotopological metaeuclidean adjacency."

"A non-logical metaphysical what?"

Wu handed me the envelope. It was covered with numbers:

$$\int_0^\infty x e^{-\Delta 3 \frac{1}{g^2}} F^2 \sqrt{\frac{\Delta \cdot dx}{\frac{1420\,mhz}{CTL}}} \cdot \frac{1?\pi}{4\Sigma c_i c_i} = \frac{H}{h}$$

"That explains the whole thing," Wu said. "A neotopological metaeuclidean adjacency. It's quite rare. In fact, I think this may be the only one."

"You're sure about this?"

"I used to be a physicist."

"I thought it was an engineer."

"Before that. Look at the figures, Irv! Numbers don't lie. That equation shows how space-time can be folded so that two parts are adjacent that are also, at the same time, separated by millions of miles. Or a quarter of a million, anyway."

"So we're talking about a sort of back door to the Moon?"

"Exactly."

On Sundays I had visitation rights to the big-screen TV. I watched golf and stock car racing all afternoon with my wife, switching back and forth during commercials. We got along a lot better now that we weren't speaking. Especially when she was holding the remote. On Monday morning, Wu arrived at the door at nine o'clock sharp, wearing coveralls and carrying a shopping bag and a toolbox.

"How do you know I don't have court today?" I asked.

"Because I know you have only one case at present, your divorce, in which you are representing both parties in order to save money. Hi, Diane."

"Hi, Wu." (She was speaking to him.)

We took my 145. Wu was silent all the way out Eastern Parkway, doing figures on a cocktail napkin from a Bay Ridge nightclub. "Go out last night?" I asked. After a whole day with Diane, I was dying to have somebody to talk to.

"Something was bothering me all night," he said. "Since the surface of the Moon is a vacuum, how come all the air on Earth doesn't rush through the shed door, along with the tires?"

"I give up," I said.

We were at a stoplight. "There it is," he said. He handed me the napkin, on which was scrawled:

$$\frac{H}{h} = \int_{WAP}^{oo} \left| \frac{1420)dx}{\Delta 33} \div \frac{1}{4\Delta (z')} \right| \int^{.32} \sqrt{RHT} \cdot \sum \frac{dx}{K\cos^2} = \frac{h}{H}$$

"There what is?"

"The answer to my question. As those figures demonstrate, Irv, we're not just dealing with a neotopological metaeuclidean adjacency. We're dealing with an *incongruent* neotopological metaeuclidean adjacency. The two areas are still separated by a quarter of a million miles, even though that distance has been folded to the width of a centimeter. It's all there in black and white. See?"

"I guess," I said. The fourth thing you learn in law school is to never admit you don't understand something.

"The air doesn't rush through, because it can't. It can kind of seep through, though, creating a slight microclimate in the immediate vicinity of the adjacency. Which is probably why we don't die immediately of decompression. A tire can roll through, if you give it a shove, but air is too, too…"

"Too wispy to shove," I said.

"Exactly."

I looked for the turn off Conduit, but nothing was familiar. I tried a few streets, but none of them led us into the Hole. "Not again!" Wu complained.

"Again!" I answered.

I went back to Boulevard. Vinnie was behind the counter today, and he remembered me (with a little prodding).

"You're not the only one having trouble finding the Hole," he said. "It's been hard to find lately."

"What do you mean, 'lately'?" Wu asked from the doorway.

"Just this last year. Every month or so it gets hard to find. I think it has to do with the Concorde. I read somewhere that the noise affects the tide, and the Hole isn't that far from Jamaica Bay, you know."

"Can you draw us a map?" I asked.

"I never took drawing," Vinnie said, "so listen up close."

Vinnie's instructions had to do with an abandoned railroad track, a wrong-way turn onto a one-way street, a dogleg that cut across a health club parking lot, and several other ins and outs. While I was negotiating all this, Wu was scrawling the back of a carwash flyer he had taken from Vinnie's counter.

"The tide," he muttered. "I should have known!"

I didn't ask him what he meant; I figured (I knew!) he would tell me. But before he had a chance, we were bouncing down a dirt track through some scruffy trees, and onto the now-familiar dirt streets of the Hole. "Want some more moon rocks?" I asked when we passed the kids and their stand.

"I'll pick up my own today, Irv!"

I pulled up by the gate and we let ourselves in. Wu carried the shopping bag; he gave me the toolbox.

The old man was working on an ancient 122, the Volvo that looks like a '48 Ford from the back. (It was always one of my favorites.) "It's electric," he said when Wu and I walked up.

"The 122?" I asked.

"The dune buggy," the old man said. "Electric is the big thing now. All the cars in California are going to be electric next year. It's the law."

"No, it's not," I said. "So what, anyway?"

"That makes that dune buggy worth a lot of money."

"No, it doesn't. Besides, you already agreed on a price."

"That's right. Five hundred," Wu said. He pulled five bills from his pocket and unfolded them.

"I said I couldn't take *less* than five hundred," the old man said. "I never said I couldn't take more."

Before Wu could answer, I pulled him behind the 122. "Remember the second thing we learned in law school!" I said. "When to walk away. We can come back next week — if you still want that thing."

Wu shook his head. "It won't be here next week. I realized

something when Vinnie told us that the Hole was getting hard to find. The adjacency is warping the neighborhood as well as the cislunar space-time continuum. And since it's lunar, it has a monthly cycle. Look at this."

He handed me the car wash flyer, on the back of which was scrawled:

$$T = \propto \frac{\sqrt{\frac{L}{G}}}{H(h)} = \frac{1}{g^2} F^2$$

"See?" said Wu. "We're not just dealing with an incongruent neotopological metaeuclidean adjacency. We're dealing with a *periodic* incongruent neotopological metaeuclidean adjacency."

"Which means..."

"The adjacency comes and goes. With the Moon."

"Sort of like PMS."

"Exactly. I haven't got the figures adjusted for daylight savings time yet, but the Moon is on the wane, and I'm pretty sure that after today, Frankie will be out of the illegal dumping business for a month, at least."

"Perfect. So we come back next month."

"Irv, I don't want to take the chance. Not with a million dollars at stake."

"Not with a what?" He had my attention.

"That LRV cost two million new, and only three of them were made. Once we get it out, all we have to do is contact

NASA. Or Boeing. Or the Air & Space Museum at the Smithsonian. But we've got to strike while the iron is hot. Give me a couple of hundred bucks and I'll give you a fourth interest."

"A half."

"A third. Plus the P1800."

"You already gave me the P1800."

"Yeah, but I was only kidding. Now I'm serious."

"Deal," I said. But instead of giving Wu two hundred, I plucked the five hundred-dollar bills out of his hand. "But you stick to the numbers. I do all the talking."

We got it for six hundred. Non-refundable. "What does that mean?" Wu asked.

"It means you boys own the dune buggy — whether you get it out of the cave or not," said the old man, counting his money.

"Fair enough," said Wu. It didn't seem fair to me at all, but I kept my mouth shut. I couldn't imagine a scenario in which we would get our money back from the old man, anyway.

He went back to work on the engine of the 122, and Wu and I headed for the far end of the yard. We found Frankie rolling tires through the shed door: *pop, pop, pop*. The pile by the fence was as big as ever. He waved and kept on working.

Wu set down the shopping bag and pulled out two of those spandex bicycling outfits. He handed one to me, and started taking off his shoes.

I'll spare you the ensuing interchange — what I said, what he said, objections, arguments, etc. Suffice it to say that, ten minutes later, I was wearing black and purple tights under my coveralls, and so was Wu. Supposedly, they were to keep our skin from blistering in the vacuum. Wu was hard to resist when he had his mind made up.

I wondered what Frankie thought of it all. He just kept rolling tires through the doorway, one by one.

There were more surprises in the bag. Wu pulled out rubber gloves and wool mittens, a brown bottle with Chinese writing on it, a roll of clear plastic vegetable bags from the supermarket, a box of cotton balls, a roll of duct tape, and a rope.

Frankie didn't say anything until Wu got to the rope. Then he stopped working, sat down on the pile of tires, lit a cigarette, and said, "Won't work."

Wu begged his pardon.

"I'll show you," Frankie said. He tied one end of the rope to a tire and tossed it through the low door into the shed. There was the usual *pop* and then a fierce crackling noise.

Smoke blew out the door. Wu and I both jumped back.

Frankie pulled the rope back, charred on one end. There was no tire. "I learned the hard way," he said, "when I tried to pull the dune buggy through myself, before I took the wheels off."

"Of course!" Wu said. "What a fool I've been. I should have known!"

"Should have known what?" Frankie and I both asked at once.

Wu tore a corner off the shopping bag and started scrawling numbers on it with a pencil stub. "Should have known this!" he said, and he handed it to Frankie.

Frankie looked at it, shrugged, and handed it to me:

$$t_p \approx \frac{1}{G} \times \frac{e^4}{mpm} = eC^3$$
$$\overline{\phantom{t_p \approx \frac{1}{G} \times \frac{e^4}{mpm} = eC^3}}$$
$$h(H)$$

"So?" I said.

"So, there it is!" Wu said. "As those figures clearly indicate, you can *pass through* a noncongruent adjacency, but you can't *connect* its two aspects. It's only logical. Imagine the differential energy stored when a quarter of a million miles of space-time is folded to less than a millimeter."

"Burns right through a rope," Frankie said.

"Exactly."

"How about a chain?" I suggested.

"Melts a chain," said Frankie. "Never tried a cable, though."

"No substance known to man could withstand that awesome energy differential," Wu said. "Not even cable. That's why the tires make that *pop*. I'll bet you have to roll them hard or they bounce back, right?"

"Whatever you say," said Frankie, putting out his cigarette. He was losing interest.

"Guess that means we leave it there," I said. I had mixed

feelings. I hated to lose a third of a million dollars, but I didn't like the looks of that charred rope. Or the smell. I was even willing to kiss my hundred bucks goodbye.

"Leave it there? No way. We'll drive it out," Wu said. "Frankie, do you have some twelve-volt batteries you can loan me? Three, to be exact."

"Unc's got some," said Frankie. "I suspect he'll want to sell them, though. Unc's not much of a loaner."

Why was I not surprised?

Half an hour later we had three twelve-volt batteries in a supermarket shopping cart. The old man had wanted another hundred dollars, but since I was now a partner I did the bargaining, and we got them for twenty bucks apiece, charged and ready to go, with the cart thrown in. Plus three sets of jumper cables, on loan.

Wu rolled the two wire mesh wheels through the shed door. Each went *pop* and was gone. He put the toolbox into the supermarket cart with the batteries and the jumper cables. He pulled on the rubber gloves, and pulled the wool mittens over them. I did the same.

"Ready, Irv?" Wu said. (I would have said no, but I knew it wouldn't do any good. So I didn't say anything.) "We won't be able to talk on the Moon, so here's the plan. First, we push the cart through. Don't let it get stuck in the doorway where it connects the two aspects of the adjacency, or it'll start to heat up. Might even explode. Blow up both worlds. Who knows?

Once we're through, you head down the hill with the cart. I'll bring the two wheels. When we get to the LRV, you pick up the front end and — "

"Don't we have a jack?"

"I'm expecting very low gravity. Besides, the LRV is lighter than a golf cart. Only four hundred and sixty pounds, and that's here on Earth. You hold it up while I mount the wheels —I have the tools laid out in the tray of the toolbox. Then you hand me the batteries, they go in front, and I'll connect them with the jumper cables, in series. Then we climb in and — "

"Aren't you forgetting something, Wu?" I said. "We won't be able to hold our breath long enough to do all that."

"Ah so!" Wu grinned and held up the brown bottle with Chinese writing on it. "No problem! I have here the ancient Chinese herbal treatment known as (he said some Chinese words), or 'Pond Explorer.' Han dynasty sages used it to lie underwater and meditate for hours. I ordered this from Hong Kong, where it is called (more Chinese words), or 'Mud Turtle Master' and used by thieves; but no matter, it's the same stuff. Hand me those cotton balls."

The bottle was closed with a cork. Wu uncorked it and poured thick brown fluid on a cotton ball; it hissed and steamed.

"Jesus," I said.

"Pond Explorer not only provides the blood with oxygen, it suppresses the breathing reflex. As a matter of fact, you *can't* breathe while it's under your tongue. Which means you can't talk. It also contracts the capillaries and slows the heartbeat. It also scours the nitrogen out of the blood so you don't get the bends."

"How do you know all this?"

"I was into organic chemistry for several years," Wu said. "Did my master's thesis on ancient Oriental herbals. Never finished it, though."

"Before you studied math?"

"After math, before law. Open up."

As he prepared to put the cotton ball under my tongue, he said, "Pond Explorer switches your cortex to an ancient respiratory pattern predating the oxygenation of the Earth's atmosphere. Pretty old stuff, Irv! It will feel perfectly natural, though. Breathe out and empty your lungs. There! When we come out, spit it out immediately so you can breathe and talk. It's that simple."

The Pond Explorer tasted bitter. I felt oxygen (or something) flooding my tongue and my cheeks. My mouth tingled. Once I got used to it, it wasn't so bad; as a matter of fact, it felt great. Except for the taste, which didn't go away.

Wu put his cotton ball under his tongue, smiled, and corked the bottle. Then, while I watched in alarm, he tore two plastic bags off the roll.

I saw what was coming. I backed away, shaking my head—

I'll spare you the ensuing interchange. Suffice it to say that, minutes later, we both had plastic bags over our heads, taped around our necks with duct tape. Once I got over my initial panic, it wasn't so bad. As always, Wu seemed to know what he was doing. And as always, it was no use resisting his plans.

If you're wondering what Frankie was making of all this, so was I. He had stopped working again. While my bag was being taped on, I saw him sitting on the pile of tires, watching us with those blue-green eyes; looking a little bored, as if he saw such goings-on every day.

It was time. Wu grabbed the front of the supermarket cart and I grabbed the handle. Wu spun his finger and pointed toward the shed door with its tattered shower curtain waving slightly in the ripples of the space-time interface. We were off!

I waved goodbye to Frankie. He lifted one finger in farewell as we ran through.

From the Earth to the Moon — in one long step for mankind (and in particular, Wilson Wu). I heard a crackling, even through the plastic bag, and the supermarket cart shuddered and shook like a lawnmower with a bent blade. Then we were on the other side, and there was only a huge cold empty silence.

Overhead, a million stars. At our feet, gray dust. The door we had come through was a dimly lighted hole under a low cliff behind us. We were looking down a gray slope strewn with tires. The flat area at the bottom of the slope was littered with empty bottles, wrappers, air tanks, a big tripod, and of course, the dune buggy — or LRV — nose down in the dust. There were tracks all around it. Beyond were low hills, gray-green except for an occasional black stone. Everything seemed close; there was no far away. Except for the tires, the junk, and the tracks around the dune buggy, the landscape was featureless, smooth. Unmarked. Untouched. Lifeless.

The whole scene was half-lit, like dirty snow under a full moon in winter, only brighter. And more green.

Wu was grinning like a mad man. His plastic bag had expanded so that it looked like a space helmet; I realized mine probably looked the same. This made me feel better.

Wu pointed up behind us. I turned, and there was the Earth—hanging in the sky like a blue-green, oversized moon, just like the cover of *The Whole Earth Catalog*. I hadn't actually doubted Wu, but I hadn't actually believed him either, until then. The fifth thing you learn in law school is to be comfortable in that "twilight zone" between belief and doubt.

Now I believed it. We were on the Moon, looking back at the Earth. And it was cold! The gloves did no good at all, even with the wool over the rubber. But there was no time to worry about it. Wu had already picked up the wire mesh wheels and started down the slope, sort of hopping with one under each arm, trying to miss the scattered tires. I followed, dragging the grocery cart behind me. I had expected it to bog down in the dust, but it didn't. The only problem was, the low gravity made it hard for me to keep my footing. I had to wedge my toes under the junk tires and pull it a few feet at a time.

The dune buggy, or LRV, as Wu liked to call it, was about the size of a jeep without a hood (or even an engine). It had two seats side by side, like lawn chairs with plastic webbing, facing a square console the size of a portable TV. Between the seats was a gearshift. There was no steering wheel. An umbrella-shaped antenna attached to the front end made the whole thing look like a contraption out of *E.T.* or *Mary Poppins.*

I picked up the front end, and Wu started putting on the left wheel, fitting it under the round fiberglass fender. Even though the LRV was light, the sudden exertion reminded me that I wasn't breathing, and I felt an instant of panic. I closed my eyes and sucked my tongue until it went away. The bitter taste of the Pond Explorer was reassuring.

When I opened my eyes, it looked like a fog was rolling in: it was my plastic bag, fogging up. I could barely see Wu, already finishing the left wheel. I wondered if he had ever worked on an Indy pit crew. (I found out later that he had.)

Wu crossed to the right wheel. The fog was getting thicker. I tried wiping it off with one hand, but of course, it was on the inside. Wu gave the thumbs up, and I set the front end down. I pointed at my plastic bag, and he nodded. His was fogged up, too. He tossed his wrench into the toolbox, and the plastic tray shattered like glass (silently, of course). Must have been the cold. My fingers and toes were killing me.

Wu started hopping up the slope, and I followed. I couldn't see the Earth overhead, or the Moon below; everything was a blur. I wondered how we would find our way out (or in?), back through the shed door. I needn't have worried. Wu took my hand and led me through, and this time I heard the *pop.* Blinking in the light, we tore the bags off our heads.

Wu spit out his cotton, and I did the same. My first breath felt strange. And wonderful. I had never realized breathing was so much fun.

There was a high-pitched cheer. Several of the neighborhood kids had joined Frankie on the pile of tires.

"Descartes," Wu said.

"We left it down there," I said.

"No, I mean our location. It's in the lunar highlands, near the equator. Apollo 16. Young, Duke, and Mattingly. Nineteen seventy-two. I recognize the battery cover on the LRV. The return was a little hairy, though. Ours, I mean, not theirs. I had to follow the tires the last few yards. We'll spray some WD-40 on the inside of the plastic bags before we go back in."

"Stuff's good for everything," Frankie said.

"Almost," I said.

It was noon, and I was starving, but there was no question of breaking for lunch. Wu was afraid the batteries would freeze; though they were Heavy Duty, they were made for Earth, not the Moon. With new Pond Explorer and new plastic bags properly treated with WD-40, we went back in. I had also taped plastic bags over my shoes. My toes were still stinging from the cold.

As we went down the slope toward the LRV site, we tossed a few of the tires aside to clear a road. With any luck, we would be coming up soon.

We left the original NASA batteries in place and set the

new (well, used, but charged) batteries on top of them, between the front fenders. While Wu hooked them up with the jumper cables, I looked around for what I hoped was the last time. There was no view, just low hills all around, the one in front of us strewn with tires like burnt donuts. The shed door (or adjacency, as Wu liked to call it) was a dimly lit cave under a low cliff at the top of the slope. It wasn't a long hill, but it was steep — about twelve degrees.

I wondered if the umbrella-antenna would make it through the door. As if he had read my mind, Wu was already unbolting it when I turned back around. He tossed it aside with the rest of the junk, sat down, and patted the seat beside him.

I climbed in, or rather "on," since there was no "in" to the LRV. Wu sat, of course, on the left. It occurred to me that if the English had been first on the Moon, he would have been on the right. There was no steering wheel or foot pedals either — but that didn't bother Wu. He seemed to know exactly what he was doing. He hit a few switches on the console, and dials lighted up for "roll," "heading," "power," etc. With a mad grin toward me, and a thumbs up toward the top of the slope (or the Earth hanging above it), he pushed the T-handle between us forward.

The LRV lurched. It groaned — I could "hear" it through my seat and my tailbone — and began to roll slowly forward. I could tell the batteries were weak.

If the LRV had lights, we didn't need them. The Earth, hanging over the adjacency like a gigantic pole star, gave plenty of light. The handle I had thought was a gearshift was actually a joystick, like on a video game. Pushing it to one side, Wu turned the LRV sharply to the right — all four wheels turned — and started up the slope.

It was slow going. You might think the Earth would have looked friendly, but it didn't. It looked cold and cruel; it seemed to be mocking us. The batteries, which had started out weak, were getting weaker. Wu's smile was gone already. The path we had cleared through the tires was useless; the LRV would never make it straight up the slope.

I climbed down and began clearing an angled switchback. If pulling things on the Moon is hard, throwing them is almost fun. I hopped from tire to tire, slinging them down the hill, while Wu drove behind me.

The problem was, even on a switchback, the corners are steep. The LRV was still twenty yards from the top when the batteries gave out entirely. I didn't hear it, of course; but when I looked back after clearing the last stretch, I saw it was stopped. Wu was banging on the joystick with both hands. His plastic bag was swollen, and I was afraid it would burst. I had never seen Wu lose it before. It alarmed me. I ran (or rather, hopped) back to help out.

I started unhooking the jumper cables. Wu stopped banging on the joystick and helped. The supermarket cart had been left at the bottom, but the batteries were light enough in the lunar gravity. I picked up one under each arm and started up the hill. I didn't bother to look back, because I knew Wu would be following with the other one.

We burst through the adjacency — the shed door —

together; we tore the plastic bags off our heads and spit out the cotton balls. Warm air flooded my lungs. It felt wonderful. But my toes and fingers were on fire.

"Damn and Hell!" Wu said. I had never heard him curse before. "We almost made it!"

"We can still make it," I said. "We only lack a few feet. Let's put these babies on the charger and get some pizza."

"Good idea," Wu said. He was calming down. "I have a tendency to lose it when I'm hungry. But look, Irv. Our problems are worse than we thought."

I groaned. Two of the batteries had split along the sides when we had set them down. All three were empty; the acid had boiled away in the vacuum of the Moon. It was a wonder they had worked at all.

"Meanwhile, are your toes hurting?" Wu asked.

"My toes are killing me," I said.

The sixth thing you learn in law school is that cash solves all (or almost all) problems. I had one last hundred-dollar bill hidden in my wallet for emergencies — and if this didn't qualify, what did? We gave the old man ninety for three more batteries, and put them on fast charge. Then we sent our change (ten bucks) with one of the kids on a bike, for four slices of pizza and two cans of diet soda.

Then we sat down under an ailanthus and took off our shoes. I was pleased to see that my toes weren't black. They warmed fairly quickly in the sun. It was my shoes that were cold. The tassel on one of my loafers was broken; the other one snapped when I touched it.

"I'm going to have to bypass some of the electrics on the LRV if we're going to make it up the hill," said Wu. He grabbed a piece of newspaper that was blowing by and began to trace a diagram. "According to my calculations, those batteries will put out 33.9 percent power for sixteen minutes if we drop out the nav. system. Or maybe shunt past the rear steering motors. Look at this—"

"I'll take your word for it," I said. "Here's our pizza."

My socks were warm. I taped two plastic bags over my feet this time, while Wu poured the Pond Explorer over the cotton balls. It steamed when it went on, and a cheer went up from the kids on the pile of tires. There were ten or twelve of them now. Frankie was charging them a quarter apiece. Wu paused before putting the cotton ball under his tongue.

"Kids," he said, "don't try this at home!"

They all hooted. Wu taped the plastic bag over my head, then over his. We waved—we were neighborhood heroes!— and picked up the "new" batteries, which were now charged; and ducked side by side back through the adjacency to the junk-strewn lunar slope where our work still waited to be finished. We were the first interplanetary automotive salvage team!

Wu was carrying two batteries this time, and I was carrying one. We didn't stop to admire the scenery. I was already sick of the Moon. Wu hooked up the batteries while I got into the passenger seat. He got in beside me and hit a few switches, fewer this time. The "heading" lights on the console didn't come on. Half the steering and drive enable switches remained unlighted.

Then Wu put my left hand on the joystick, and jumped down and grabbed the back of the LRV, indicating that he was going to push. I was going to drive.

I pushed the joystick forward and the LRV groaned into action, a little livelier than last time. The steering was slow; only the front wheels turned. I was hopeful, though. The LRV groaned through the last curve without slowing down.

I headed up the last straightaway, feeling the batteries weaken with every yard, every foot, every inch. It was as if the weight that had been subtracted from everything else on the Moon had been added to the LRV and was dragging it down. The lights on the console were flickering.

We were only ten yards from the adjacency. It was a dim slot under the cliff; I knew it was bright on the other side (a midsummer afternoon!), but apparently the same interface that kept the air from leaking through also dimmed the light.

It looked barely wide enough. But low. I was glad the LRV didn't have a windshield. I would have to duck to make it through.

Fifteen feet from the opening. Ten. Eight. The LRV stopped. I jammed the joystick forward and it moved another foot. I reached back over the seat and jiggled the jumper cables.

The LRV groaned forward another six inches — then died. I looked at the slot under the cliff just ahead, and at the Earth overhead, both equally far away.

I wiggled the joystick. Nothing. I started to get down to help push, but Wu stopped me. He had one more trick. He unhooked the batteries and reversed their order. It shouldn't have made any difference but as I have often noticed, electrical matters are not logical, like law: Things that shouldn't work, often do.

Sometimes, anyway. I jammed the joystick all the way forward again.

The LRV groaned forward again, and groaned on. I pointed it into the slot and ducked. I saw a shimmering light, and I felt the machine shudder. The front of the LRV poked through the shower curtain into the sunlight, and I followed, the sudden heat making my plastic bag swell.

The batteries groaned their last. I jumped down and began to pull on the front bumper. Through the plastic bag I could hear the kids screaming; or were they cheering? There was a loud crackling sound from behind the shower curtain. The LRV was only halfway through, and the front end was jumping up and down.

I tore the bag off my head and spit out the cotton, then took a deep breath and yelled, "Wu!"

I heard a hiss and a crackling; I could feel the ground shake under my feet. The pile of tires was slowly collapsing behind me; kids were slipping and sliding, trying to get away. I could hear glass breaking somewhere. I yelled, "Wu!"

The front of the LRV suddenly pulled free, throwing me (not to put too fine a point on it) flat on my ass.

The ground stopped shaking. The kids cheered.

Only the front of the LRV had come through. It was burned in half right behind the seat; cut through as if by a sloppy welder. The sour smell of electrical smoke was in the air. I took a deep breath and ducked toward the curtain, after Wu. But there was no curtain there, and no shed — only a pile of loose boards.

"Wu!" I yelled. But there he was, lying on the ground among the boards. He sat up and tore the bag off his head. He spit out his cotton and took a deep breath — and looked around and groaned.

The kids were all standing and cheering. (Kids love destruction.) Even Frankie looked pleased. But the old man wasn't; he came around the corner of the garage, looking fierce. "What the Hell's going on here?" he asked. "What happened to my shed?"

"Good question," said Wu. He stood up and started tossing aside the boards that had been the shed. The shower curtain was under them, melted into a stiff plastic rag. Under it was a pile of ash and cinders — and that was all. No cave, no hole; no rear end of the LRV. No moon.

"The cave gets bigger and smaller every month," said Frankie. "But it never did that, not since it first showed up."

"When was that?" asked Wu.

"About six months ago."

"What about my jumper cables?" said the old man.

46

*

We paid him for the jumper cables with the change from the pizza, and then called a wrecker to tow our half-LRV back to Park Slope. While we were waiting for the wrecker, I pulled Wu aside. "I hope we didn't put them out of business," I said. I'm no bleeding heart liberal, but I was concerned.

"No, no," he said. "The adjacency was about to drop into a lower neotopological orbit. We just helped it along a little. It's hard to figure without an almanac, but according to the tide table for June (which I'm glad now I bothered to memorize) the adjacency won't be here next month. Or the month after. It was just here for six months, like Frankie said. It was a temporary thing, cyclical as well as periodic."

"Sort of like the Ice Ages."

"Exactly. It always occurs somewhere in this hemisphere, but usually not in such a convenient location. It could be at the bottom of Lake Huron. Or in midair over the Great Plains, as one of those unexplained air bumps."

"What about the other side of it?" I asked. "Is it always a landing site? Or was that just a coincidence?"

"Good question!" Wu picked up one of the paper plates left over from the pizza and started scrawling on it with a pencil stub. "If I take the mean lunar latitude of all six Apollo sites, and divide by the coefficient of..."

"It was just curiosity," I said. "Here's the wrecker."

We got the half-LRV towed for half-price (I did the negotiating), but we never did make our million dollars. Boeing was in Chapter Eleven; NASA was under a procurement freeze; the Air & Space Museum wasn't interested in anything that rolled.

"Maybe I should take it on the road," Wu told me after several weeks of trying. "I could be a shopping-center attraction: 'Half a Chinaman exhibits half a Lunar Roving Vehicle. Kids and adults half-price.'"

Wu's humor masked bitter disappointment. But he kept trying. The JPL (Jet Propulsion Laboratory) wouldn't accept his calls. General Motors wouldn't return them. Finally, the Huntsville Parks Department, which was considering putting together an Apollo Memorial, agreed to send their Assistant Administrator for Adult Recreation to have a look.

She arrived on the day my divorce became final. Wu and I met her in the garage, where I had been living while Diane and I were waiting to sell the house. Her eyes were big and blue-green, like Frankie's. She measured the LRV and shook her head. "It's like a dollar bill," she said.

"How's that?" Wu asked. He looked depressed. Or maybe skeptical. It was getting hard to tell the difference.

"If you have over half, it's worth a whole dollar. If you have less than half, it's worth nothing. You have slightly less than half of the LRV here, which means that it is worthless. What'll you take for that old P1800, though? Isn't that the one that was assembled in England?"

Which is how I met Candy. But that's another story.

*

We closed on the house two days later. Since the garage went with it, I helped Wu move the half-LRV to his backyard, where it sits to this day. It was lighter than any motorcycle. We moved the P1800 (which had plates) onto the street, and on Saturday morning, I went to get the interior for it. Just as Wu had predicted, the Hole was easy to find now that it was no longer linked with the adjacency. I didn't even have to stop at Boulevard Imports. I just turned off Conduit onto a likely looking street, and there it was.

The old man would hardly speak to me, but Frankie was understanding. "Your partner came out and gave me this," he said. He showed me a yellow legal pad, on which was scrawled:

$$H\left(M = \frac{E}{c^2}\right)h$$

"He told me this explains it all, I guess."

Frankie had stacked the boards of the shed against the garage. There was a cindery bare spot where the shed door had been; the cinders had that sour moon smell. "I was sick and tired of the tire disposalment business, anyway," Frankie confided in a whisper.

The old man came around the corner of the garage. "What happened to your buddy?" he asked.

"He's going to school on Saturday mornings," I said. Wu

was studying to be a meteorologist. I was never sure if that was weather or shooting stars. Anyway, he had quit the law.

"Good riddance," said the old man.

The old man charged me sixty-five dollars for the interior panels, knobs, handles, and trim. I had no choice but to pay up. I had the money, since I had sold Diane my half of the furniture. I was ready to start my new life. I didn't want to own anything that wouldn't fit into the tiny, heart-shaped trunk of the P1800.

That night, Wu helped me put in the seats, then the panels, knobs, and handles. We finished at midnight and it didn't look bad, even though I knew the colors would look weird in the daylight—blue and white in a red car. Wu was grinning that mad grin again; it was the first time I had seen it since the Moon. He pointed over the rooftops to the east (toward Howard Beach, as a matter of fact). The Moon was rising. I was glad to see it looking so—far away.

Wu's wife brought us some leftover wedding cake. I gave him the keys to the 145 and he gave me the keys to the P1800. "Guess we're about even," I said. I put out my hand, but Wu slapped it aside and gave me a hug instead, lifting me off the ground. Everybody should have a friend like Wilson Wu.

I followed the full Moon all the way to Alabama.

The Edge of the Universe

The biggest difference I have noticed
so far between the north and the South
(they insist on capitalizing it) is the
vacant lot; or maybe I should say, the
Vacant Lot. Vacant lots in Brooklyn are
grim, unappealing stretches of rubble
grown over with nameless malevolent,
malodorous plants; littered with roach-
spotted household junk; and inhabited

by scabrous, scrofulous, scurrying things you wouldn't want to look at unless it were out of the corner of an eye, in passing. Vacant lots here in Alabama, even in downtown Huntsville where I live and work (if study can be called work, and if what I do can be called study), are like miniature Euell Gibbons memorials of rustic runaway edibles and roadside ornamentals — dock and pigweed, thistle and cane, poke and honeysuckle, ragweed and wisteria — in which the odd overturned grocery cart or transmission bellhousing, the occasional sprung mattress or dead dog, the tire half-filled with black water, is an added attraction: a seasoning, you might say, that adds to rather than detracts from the charm of the flora. You would never cut through a vacant lot in Brooklyn unless you were being chased by a scarier than usual thug; in Alabama I cut across the same corner lot every day on my way from Whipper Will's law office, where I slept and studied for the bar, to Hoppy's Good Gulf where I had my own key to the men's room. I actually looked forward to my sojourns across the path and through the weeds. It was my closest regular contact with nature; or maybe I should say, Nature.

And Nostalgia, too.

One of the odd items of junk in the lot was a beaded seat cushion, of the kind much favored by New York cab drivers (particularly those from Pakistan) back in the late 1980s, and still seen occasionally. This one had known better days, and all that was left were fifty or so large wooden beads strung together by twisted neoprene line in a rough sketch, as it were, of a seat; but it was enough to make it recognizable and to give me a warm hit of the Big Apple when I saw it two or three times a day. It was like hearing a horn honk or smelling a bagel. It lay half-on and half-off the narrow red dirt path that was my route to Hoppy's Good Gulf. I watched it gradually disintegrate, becoming every week a little less recognizable, but still familiar, like a neighborhood (or a friend) in decline. I looked forward to stepping over it several times a day, for much as I loved Candy (still do — we're almost Mr. and Mrs. now!), and was getting to *like* (at least) Alabama, I missed New York. We Brooklynites are urban animals, and what could be less urban than these faded little red brick Southern "downtowns," deserted by both people and cars? I suspect they were always somewhat sad and empty, but nowadays they are sadder and emptier than ever. Like most American towns, north *and* South, Huntsville has seen its life blood flow from the old downtown to the Bypass; from the still, dark heart to the tingling, neon-lit, encircling skin of strip malls and fast food restaurants and convenience stores and discount centers.

Not that I'm complaining. Dead as it was, downtown suited me better than the Bypass, which is no place for a man on foot, which is what I was then: which is a whole other story, but one that might as well be told here, since it, too, is about Whipper Will, about an Edge (of town, not the Universe)—

And about a U-turn.

When I moved down here from Brooklyn to be with Candy, I had sold her the Volvo P1800 I acquired from my best friend

53

Wilson Wu in return for helping him bring the LRV (Lunar Roving Vehicle) back from the Moon (which is also a whole other story, and one that I've told in "The Hole in the Hole"). I helped Candy maintain the car not only because I was her boyfriend — her soon-to-be-fiancé, in fact — but because the P1800, Volvo's first and only true sports car, is a rare classic with precious idiosyncrasies that not even a Southern shade tree mechanic (and the breed has no greater admirer than I) can be expected to understand. The carburetors, for example. The Volvo's twin slide-type SUs begin to leak air after a few hundred thousand miles, and according to Wu (and he showed me the math on this — of course!), the only way to get them in synch, especially after a move to another climate, is to run the Volvo up to 4725 rpm in third gear on a four- to six-percent grade on a day approaching the local humidic mean (temperature not a factor), and lean them out in eighth-turn stages, alternating between one and the other, until the exhaust note makes a twelve-inch tinfoil pie plate wedged between the frame and the transmission case sing the note A. I don't have perfect pitch but I was able to borrow one of those little C-cell powered guitar tuners, and there is a long six-percent grade on the old four-lane at the north edge of Huntsville, where it crosses the city limits and heads around the shoulder of Squirrel Ridge, the thirteen-hundred-foot Appalachian remnant that dominates the northern half of the county. Since Wu's procedure requires several passes, I went early on a Sunday morning when I knew the city cops would all be in church, and (my first mistake) used the NO

U-TURN; FOR POLICE ONLY cut-across just past the city limits to shorten my way back down. I was finished, and getting ready to take the car back into town and pick up Candy at church (Methodist) when the ash-gray "smokey" dove out of the sun, as it were, and pounced.

Police in general, and Alabama State Troopers in particular, are humorless, excessively conventional creatures, and my second mistake was trying to explain to him that I was not actually *driving* but *tuning* the car. He used my own words to charge me with six counts of the same moving violation (Illegal U-turn). My third mistake was explaining that I was Whipper Will Knoydart's soon-to-be (for I had not yet officially proposed to Candy, for reasons which will become clear) affianced son-in-law. How was I to know that Whipper Will had once taken a shot at this particular trooper? The result of all these errors was that I was summarily hauled before a Justice of the Peace (church was just letting out), who let me know that Whipper Will had once called him a –––––––, and who then snatched away my New York driver's license and imposed a punitive three-month wait before I was eligible to apply for an Alabama license.

All of which is to explain why the P1800 was running so well; why I was on foot; and why Candy and I met for lunch in Huntsville's old downtown every (or almost every) day instead of out on the Bypass, near the Parks Department office, where she worked. It suited me fine. A New Yorker, even a car-loving Brooklynite like me, is happy on foot, and I loathe and despise the Bypass. I went through the same routine every morning: Wake up, cross the corner lot to Hoppy's Good Gulf men's room ("It's Whipper Will's Yank"), then head back to the office to wait for the mail.

I didn't even have to open it; just log it in. Whipper Will Knoydart had been a trailer park landlord for six decades, running low-rent, high-crime operations in four counties and making more enemies and fewer friends than any other man in northern Alabama. It was characteristic of the old man that his office was downtown, since he had often boasted that he wouldn't be caught dead in a mobile home, which was only suitable (according to him) for "rednecks, niggers, and –––––––s." Because Whipper Will had retired under a financial and legal cloud — a bank of clouds, actually — his office had been sealed and secured pending a state investigation. Under the agreement worked out among the Realtor's Board, the IRS, the BATF, the DEA, and several other even less savory agencies, the premises had to be overseen by an out-of-state lawyer with no pending cases, past encounters, or conflicting interests. The fact that I was crazy in love with Whipper Will's only child wasn't considered an interest: In fact, it was Candy who had recommended me for the position. Nobody else wanted it, even though the resentment of Whipper Will was softening as it sometimes softens for malefactors after they are gone. Whipper Will wasn't dead, but between Alzheimer's, prostate cancer, emphysema, and Parkinson's he was definitely fading away. He had been in the nursing home for almost nine months.

In return for answering the phone (which only rang when

Candy called) and logging in the mail, I got to use the office as a place to "live" (sleep) and study for the Alabama bar. Or at least, spread out my books; or rather, book. The problem with studying was, it was a golden Alabama October, and fall is (I have discovered) the season of love for forty-somethings. I was forty-one. I'm a little older than that now, and if you think that's self-evident, it's because you haven't heard my story, which begins on the morning I noticed that the beaded seat cushion in the vacant lot was getting better instead of worse.

It was a Tuesday, a typical, that is to say beautiful, Alabama October morning. The leaves were just beginning to think about beginning to turn. Candy and I had been out late, parking at the Overlook on Squirrel Ridge, where I had unbuttoned all but the last little button on her uniform blouse before she stopped me with that firm but gentle touch on the back of my hand that I love so much. I had slept late, entangled in the most delicious dreams, and it was almost ten before I dragged myself off the leather couch I called a bed and stumbled, half-blind, across the corner lot to Hoppy's Good Gulf.

"Whipper Will's Yank," said Hoppy, combining greeting, comment, and conversation into his usual laconic phrase. Hoppy wasn't much of a talker.

"Right," I said, which was the only answer I had been able to devise.

" 'Nuff said," he said, which was his way of signing off.

On my way back across the corner lot I stepped carefully over my old friend, the beaded seat cushion, which lay in its usual place, half-on and half-off the path. Loose beads were scattered in the dirt and grass around the neoprene strings that had once held them; it was like the reversed body of a beast whose skeleton (string) was less substantial than its flesh (beads). Perhaps it was the morning light (I thought), perhaps the dew hadn't yet dried off: But I noticed that the discarded seat cushion looked, or seemed to look, a little *better* rather than a little worse that morning.

It was weird. It was jarring because it was, after all, October, with the slow, quiet, golden process of ruin evident all around; and to me, that October, there was something personally gratifying about decline and decay, which was freeing up the woman I wanted to marry. Candy had agreed the night before up on Squirrel Ridge that, since her father was finally and securely ensconced in the nursing home, it was time to think about getting married. Or at least engaged. Sometime in the next week, I knew, she was going to allow me to propose. With all the privileges that entailed.

I decided it was my imagination (or perhaps my mood) that saw the beads reassembling themselves into a seat cushion. As always, I was careful not to kick them as I went on my way. Who was I to interfere with the processes of Nature? Back at the office I found two messages on Whipper Will's ancient reel-to-reel answering machine: one from my best friend Wilson Wu announcing that he had located the Edge of the Universe, and one from Candy informing me that she would be twenty minutes late for lunch at the "Bonny Bag." This second message worried me a little, since I could tell from the low moaning in the background that she was at Squirrel Ridge (the nursing home, not the mountain). I couldn't return either call since I didn't have outgoing, so I opened a Caffeine-Free Diet Cherry Coke from Whipper Will's old-fashioned kerosene-powered office refrigerator, spread my *Corcoran's Alabama Case Law Review* on the windowsill, and fell to my studies. When I woke up it was 12:20, and I panicked for a moment, thinking I was late for lunch. Then I remembered Candy was going to be late, too.

The Bonny Baguette is a little sandwich shop much favored by lawyers and real estate people, most of whom tend to be old-line Huntsville folks who leave the Bypass to the NASA and university types. "I was worried," I said as Candy and I both slid into the booth at the same time. "I could tell you were calling from Squirrel Ridge, and I was afraid that…"

Candy looked, as always, spectacular in her neatly pressed Parks Department khakis. Some girls are pretty without meaning to be. Candy has to work at it, and that makes her (for me) even more special, especially after having a wife who pretended, but only pretended, to despise her own beauty. But that's a whole other story. "Don't worry," Candy answered, cutting me off with that smile that had enticed me to Alabama in the first place, and a touch on the back of my hand that reminded me of our almost-intimacies of the night before. "I just had to sign something, that's all. A docu-

59

ment. A formality. A DNR, in fact."

I knew what a DNR was. A Do-Not-Resuscitate order.

"It's part of the process and everything, but still, it's weird, you know?" Candy said. "It hurts. You're telling them — ordering them — not to keep your Daddy alive. To let him die."

"Candy — " It was my turn to take her hand. "Your father is ninety years old. He's got Alzheimer's. He's got cancer. His hair is white as snow. He's got no teeth left. He's had a nice life, but now…"

"Eighty-nine," Candy said. "Daddy wasn't quite sixty when I was born, and he hasn't had a nice life. He's had a terrible life. He's been a terrible man. He's made life miserable for people in four counties. But still, he's…"

"He's not terrible anymore," I said. Which was true. I had never met the Whipper Will everybody hated. The man I knew was gentle and befuddled. He spent his days watching TNN and CMTV, perpetually smoothing a paper napkin across his knee as if he were petting a little white dog. "He's a sweet old man now, and his worries are pretty much over. It's your turn to have a nice life. Mine too. Which reminds me — I got a phone call from Wu! Something about that astronomy project he's working on."

"Wonderful," Candy said. She loved Wu; everybody loves Wu. "Where is he? Still in Hawaii?"

"Guess so," I said. "He didn't leave a number. Not that it matters, since I don't have outgoing."

"I'm sure he'll call back," said Candy.

At the Bonny Baguette, you don't order when you want to; you are called on, just like in grade school. Bonnie, the owner, comes over herself, with a little blackboard on which there are five kinds of sandwich, the same every day. Actually, grade school was never that bad; they called on you but they never brought the blackboard to your desk.

"How's your Daddy?" Bonnie asked.

"The same," said Candy. "I was out to Squirrel Ridge today — the nursing home — and they all agree he's just become the sweetest thing." She didn't say anything about the DNR.

"Amazed, I'm sure," said Bonnie. "Did I ever tell you about the time he took a shot at my Daddy? Out at Squirrel Ridge Trailer Park."

"Yes, Bonnie, you've told me, several times, but he's gotten sweeter with Alzheimer's," said Candy. "It makes some old people mean, but it made my Daddy sweet, so what can I say?"

"He also took a shot at my half brother, Earl, out at Willow Bend Trailer Park," said Bonnie. "Called him a -------."

"We should probably go ahead and order," said Candy, "since I only get fifty-five minutes for lunch, and almost eleven are gone."

"Well, of course." Bonnie sucked her cheeks and tapped her little blackboard, ready to make chalk marks. "What'll you two lovebirds have?"

I ordered the roast beef, as usual; Candy ordered the chicken salad, as usual. Each comes with a bag of chips and I got to eat both bags, as usual. "Did you hear how she called us lovebirds?" I whispered. "What say we make it official tonight? I propose I propose."

"Bonnie calls everybody lovebirds."

Candy's a sweet, old-fashioned Southern girl, a type I find fascinating because they almost never (contrary to myth) blush. She had her own reasons for being reluctant to allow me to propose (with all the privileges that entails). The last time Candy had been engaged, almost ten years before, Whipper Will had shown up drunk at the wedding rehearsal and taken a shot at the groom and then at the preacher, calling them both –––––––s, and effectively canceling the wedding and ending the engagement as well. Candy didn't want to even *hear* a proposal again until she was sure she could accept it without worrying about her old man and what he might do.

"Things are quiet, Candy. He's settled into the nursing home," I said. "We can get on with our life together. We can make plans. We can..."

"Soon," she said, touching my wrist lightly, gently, perfectly! "But not tonight. It's Wednesday, and on Wednesday nights we go 'grazing,' remember?"

I was in no hurry to get back to the office and study for the bar, so after Candy went back to work I stopped by the station and watched Hoppy replace the front brake pads on a Ford Taurus.

"Whipper Will's Yank," he said, as always.

And, as always, I replied, "Right."

But today Hoppy was in a mood for conversation, and he asked, "How's old Whipper Will?"

"Just fine," I said. "Mellow. Good as gold. He just watches CMTV and TNN all day out at Squirrel Ridge. The nursing home."

"Ever tell you about the time he took a shot at me? At Sycamore Springs Trailer Park. Called me a –––––––."

"Seems he took a shot at everybody," I said.

"Lucky he was such a bad shot," Hoppy said. "For a trailer park landlord, anyway. Meanest son of a bitch in four counties."

"Well, he's not mean anymore," I said. "He just watches CMTV and TNN all day out at Squirrel Ridge. The nursing home."

"Thank God for Alzheimer's," Hoppy said. " 'Nuff said."

He went back to work on the brakes and I strolled out into the sun and across the corner lot toward the office. I was in no hurry to start studying, so I stopped for a look at the broken-down beaded seat cushion, my little reminder of New York City. It definitely looked better. But how could that be? I knelt down and, without touching anything, counted the beads on the fourth string down from what had been in better days, the top. There were nine wooden beads; judging by the length of the naked neoprene string, it looked like another five or six had gotten away. I wrote 9 on the back of my hand with my ballpoint, feeling almost virtuous. Next time I would *know*. I would have *evidence*. I was beginning to feel like a lawyer again.

Back at the office, I took a Caffeine-Free Diet Cherry Coke out of the little refrigerator which was still crowded with Whipper Will's moonshine in pint jars. I never could figure out why he kept moonshine refrigerated. I could only guess that he didn't want to take a chance on it aging and getting better.

I spread my *Corcoran's Alabama Case Law Review* on the windowsill and fell to studying. When I woke up, the phone was ringing.

It was Wu. "Wu!"

"Didn't you get my message?" he asked.

"I did, and it's great to hear from you, finally, but I couldn't call back," I said. "I don't have outgoing. How's the family?" Wu and his wife have two boys.

"They're back in Brooklyn. Couldn't take the weather."

"In Hawaii?!?"

"I'm at the Mauna Kea Observatory," Wu said. "We're at twelve thousand feet. It's like Tibet."

"Whatever," I said. "Well, how's business? Observe any meteors lately?"

"Remember what I told you, Irving?" Wu hardly ever calls me Irving; it usually means he's irritated. "Meteorology is not about meteors. It's about weather. My job is scheduling the observatory's viewings, which depend on the weather."

"So—how's the weather, Wu?"

"Great!" Wu dropped his voice. "Which is how come we found what I told you about." He dropped his voice further. "The Edge of the Universe."

"Congratulations," I said. I didn't know it had been lost. "But why is it such a big secret?"

"Because of the implications. Unexpected, to say the least. Turns out we've had it in our sights for almost a month but didn't realize it because it was the wrong color."

"The wrong color?"

"The wrong color," said Wu. "You know about Hubble's constant, the red shift, the expanding Universe, right?" Wu asked with such confidence that I couldn't bear to let him down.

"Sure," I said.

"Well, the Universe has stopped expanding." After a pause, he added in a whisper: "In fact, according to my calculations, it's starting to shrink. What's your fax number? I'll shoot you the figures."

Whipper Will had Huntsville's—maybe even Alabama's—first fax machine. About the size of an upright piano, and not entirely electrical, it sat in the far corner of the office, against a wall where it was vented to the alley through a system of stovepipe and flex hose. I had always been reluctant to look behind its plywood sides, or under its duraluminum hood, but I understood from Hoppy (who had been called in once to fix it) that its various components were powered by an intricate and never since duplicated combination of batteries and 110, clockwork, gravity, water pressure, propane, and charcoal (for the thermal printer). No one knew who had made it, or when. I didn't even know it worked until, seconds after I gave Wu the number, I heard a relay click, and the upright fax began to groan; it began to whine. It clanked and clattered, it sputtered and roared, it spat cold steam and warm gases, and a paper fell out of the wicker IN bin, onto the floor.

It was smeared with purple stains, which I recognized from grade school as mimeo ink, and it bore a formula in Wu's hand:

$$\int_{\infty}^{0} H = \frac{(2\pi\,^{m}e)^{\frac{3}{4}}}{a/4^{?}} e\sqrt{\frac{\angle\,\|\,^{m}Z}{-\frac{1}{K?'}}}$$

"What's this?" I asked.

"Just what it looks like. Hubble's constant inconstant: reversed, confused, confounded," Wu said. "You'll note that the red shift has turned to blue, just like in the Elvis song."

"That's blue to gold," I said. "'When My Blue Moon Turns to Gold Again.'"

"Irving, this is more important than any Elvis song!" he said (rather self-righteously, I thought, since it was he who had brought up Elvis in the first place). "It means that the Universe has stopped expanding and started to collapse in on itself."

"I see," I lied. "Is that—good or bad?"

"Not good," Wu said. "It's the beginning of the end. Or at least the end of the beginning. The period of expansion that began with the Big Bang is over, and we're on our way to the Big Crunch. It means the end of life as we know it; Hell, of existence as we know it. Everything in the Universe, all the stars, all the planets, all the galaxies — the Earth and everything on it from the Himalayas to the Empire State Building to the Musée d'Orsay — will be squashed into a lump about the size of a tennis ball."

"That does sound bad," I said. "When's this Crunch thing going to happen?"

"It will take a while."

"What's 'a while'?" I couldn't help thinking of Candy, and our plans to get married (even though I hadn't yet officially proposed).

"Eleven to fifteen billion years," said Wu. "By the way, how's Candy? Are you two engaged yet?"

"Almost," I said. "We're going 'grazing' tonight. As soon as her father's settled in the nursing home, I get to pop the question."

"Congratulations," Wu said. "Or maybe I should say pre-congratula — Whoooops! Here comes my boss. I'm not supposed to be using this line. Give my best to Candy. What's 'grazing' anyway…?"

But before I could answer, he was gone. Everybody should have a friend like Wilson Wu. He grew up in Queens and studied physics at Bronx Science, pastry in Paris, math at Princeton, herbal medicine in Hong Kong, and law at either Harvard or Yale (I get them confused). He worked for NASA (Boeing, anyway), then Legal Aid. Did I mention that he's six-foot-two and plays guitar? We lived on the same block in Brooklyn where we both owned Volvos and went to the Moon. Then I met Candy and moved to Alabama, and Wu quit Legal Aid and got a degree in meteorology.

Which is *not* about meteors.

The Saturn Five SixPlex, in the Apollo Shopping Center on the Huntsville Bypass, with its half-dozen identical theaters half-guarded by bored teens, is perfect for "grazing," an activity invented by Candy and her friends some fifteen years ago, when the multiplexes first started hitting the suburbs of the bigger Southern towns. The idea, initially, was to make dating more flexible, since teen girls and boys rarely liked the same movies. Later, as Candy and her friends matured and movies continued their decline, the idea was to combine several features into one full-featured (if you will) film. When you go "grazing" you wear several sweaters and hats, using them to stake out seats and to change your appearance as you duck from theater to theater. Dates always sit together when in the same theater, but "grazing" protocol demands that you never pressure your date into staying — or leaving. Boys and girls come and go as they wish, sometimes together, sometimes apart. That Wednesday night there was a teen sex comedy, a tough-love ladies' weeper, a lawyer-in-jeopardy thriller, a buddy cop romance, a singing animal musical cartoon, and a terror thug "blow-'em-up." The films didn't run in the same time continuum, of course, and

Candy and I liked to "graze" backward; we began with the car bombs and angled back across the hall (and across Time) for the courtroom confession, then split up for the singing badgers (me) and Whoopi's teary wisecracks (Candy) before coming together for the teens' nervous first kiss. "Grazing" always reminds me of the old days before movies became an art, when "the picture show" in Brooklyn ran in a continuous loop and no one ever worried about Beginnings or Endings. You stayed till you got to the part where you came in, then it was over. "'Grazing' is a lot like marriage, don't you think?" I whispered.

"Marriage?" Candy asked, alarmed. We were together, watching the cops question a landlady. "Are you pressuring me?"

"I'm not proposing," I said. "I'm making a comment."

"Comments about movies are allowed. Comments about marriage are considered pressuring."

"My comment is about 'grazing,'" I said. "It's about..."

"Sssshhhh!" said the people behind us.

I lowered my voice. "...about being together some of the time and apart some of the time. About entering together and leaving together. About being free to follow your own tastes yet always conscious that there is a seat saved for you beside the other."

I was crazy about her. "I'm crazy about you," I whispered.

"Sssshhhh!" said the couple behind us.

"Tomorrow night," Candy whispered, taking my hand.

Then she held it up so that it was illuminated by the head-lights of a car chase. "What's this?" She was looking at the number on the back of my hand.

"That's there to — remind me of how much I love you," I lied. I didn't want to tell her what it really was; I didn't want her to think I was crazy.

"Only six?"

"You're holding it upside down."

"That's better!"

"Ow!"

"Ssssshhhhhh!" said the couple behind us.

We skipped all the titles and credits but caught all the previews. Candy dropped me off at midnight at the Good Gulf men's room. Walking "home" to Whipper Will's office across the corner lot, I looked up at the almost-full Moon and thought of Wu on his Hawaiian mountaintop. There were only a few stars; maybe the Universe *was* shrinking. Wu's figures, though I could never understand them, were usually right. What did I care, though? A few billion years can seem like eternity when you're young, and forty-one isn't old. A second marriage can be like a second youth. I stepped carefully over my old friend, the beaded seat cushion, which looked better than ever in the moonlight; but then, don't we all?

It was almost ten o'clock before I awoke the next morning. I made my way to Hoppy's Good Gulf, staggering a little in the sunshine. "Whipper Will's Yank," Hoppy said from the repair bay where he was replacing the front brake pads on another Taurus.

"Right," I muttered.

He replied "'Nuff said" behind me, as I made my way back outside and started across the corner lot.

I stopped at the beaded seat cushion. It definitely looked better. There seemed to be fewer loose beads scattered in the weeds and on the path. There seemed to be fewer naked, broken neoprene strings and bare spots on the seat cushion.

But I didn't have to guess. I had evidence.

I checked the number on the back of my hand: 9.

I counted the beads four rows down from the top: eleven.

I checked both again, and again it came out the same.

It was creepy. I looked around in the bushes, half expecting to see giggling boys playing a joke on me. Or even Hoppy. But the bushes were empty. This was downtown on a school day. No kids played in this corner lot anyway.

I spit on my thumb and rubbed out the 9, and walked on back to the office. I was hoping to find another message from Wu, but there was nothing on the machine.

It was only ten-thirty, and I wasn't going to see Candy until lunch at the Bonny Bag, so I opened a can of Caffeine-Free Diet Cherry Coke and spread out my *Corcoran's*. I was just starting to doze off when Whipper Will's ancient upright fax machine clicked twice and wheezed into life; it sputtered and shuddered, it creaked and it clanked, it hissed and whistled, and then spat a smeared-purple mimeo sheet on the floor, covered with figures:

$$\frac{Q}{H} = \frac{17\pi}{\Delta \cdot dx} \left(\frac{c400}{WAP}\right)_N^4 \sum_{-kT} \left. \frac{dx}{cos5 \frown}\right/_{\triangle 33} \infty$$

As soon as it cooled, I picked it up and smoothed it out. I was just about to put it with the other one when the phone rang.

"Well?" It was Wu.

"More Big Crunch?" I was guessing, of course.

"You must be holding it upside down," Wu said. "The figures I just sent are for the Anti-Entropic Reversal."

"So I see," I lied. "Does this reversal mean there won't be a Big Crunch after all?" I wasn't surprised; it had always sounded more like a breakfast cereal than a disaster.

"Irving!" Wu said. "Look at the figures more closely. The AER leads up to the Big Crunch; it *makes* it happen. The Universe doesn't just shrink, it rewinds. It goes backwards. According to my calculations, everything will be running in reverse for the next eleven to fifteen billion years, from now until the Big Crunch. Trees will grow from ashes to firewood to oak to seed. Broken glass will fly together into windowpanes. Tea will get hot in the cup."

"Sounds interesting," I said. "Could even be handy. When does all this happen?"

"It's already started," said Wu. "The Anti-Entropic Reversal is going on right now."

"Are you sure?" I felt my Caffeine-Free Diet Cherry Coke. It was getting warmer, but shouldn't it be getting colder? Then I looked at the clock. It was almost eleven. "Things aren't going backward here," I said.

"Of course not, not yet," Wu said. "It begins at the Edge of the Universe. It's like a line of traffic starting up, or the tide turning; first it has to take up the slack, so in the beginning it will seem like nothing is happening. At what point does the tide turn? We may not notice anything for several thousand years. A blink of the eye in cosmic time."

I blinked. I couldn't help thinking of the beaded seat cushion. "But wait. Is it possible that something here *could* already be going backward?" I asked. "Rewinding?"

"Not very likely," Wu said. "The Universe is awfully big, and…"

Just then I heard a knock. "Gotta go," I said. "There's somebody at the door."

It was Candy, in her trim Parks Department khakis. Instead of giving me, her soon-to-be-fiancé, a kiss, she walked straight to the little kerosene-powered office refrigerator and opened a Caffeine-Free Diet Cherry Coke. I knew right away that something was wrong because Candy loathes and despises Caffeine-Free Diet Cherry Coke.

"Aren't we meeting for lunch?" I asked.

"I got a call a few minutes ago," she said. "From Squirrel Ridge, the nursing home. Daddy hit Buzzer."

I tried to look grave; I tried to hide my guilty smile. In my wishful thinking I thought I had heard "hit the buzzer," and figured it was a local variant of "kick the bucket." I crossed the room and took Candy's hand. "I'm so sorry," I lied.

"You're not half as sorry as Buzzer is," Candy said, already dragging me toward the door. "He's the one with the black eye."

Squirrel Ridge, the nursing home, sits in a hollow just north and east of Huntsville, overlooked by Squirrel Ridge, the mountain. It's a modern, single-story establishment that looks like a grade school or a motel, but smells like — well, like what it is. The smell hits you as soon as you walk in the door: a dismaying mix of ordure and disorder, urine and perfume, soft food and damp towels, new vomit and old sheets, Beech-Nut and Lysol pine. Next, the sounds hit you: scuffing slippers, grunts and groans, talk-show applause, the ring of dropping bedpans, the creak of wire-spoke wheels — broken by an occasional panicked shout or soul-chilling scream. It sounds as if a grim struggle is being fought at intervals, while daily life shuffles on around it. And indeed it is. A struggle to the death.

I followed Candy to the end of a long hall, where we found her father in the dayroom, smiling sweetly, strapped in a chair in front of a TV watching Alan Jackson sing and pretend to play the guitar. "Good morning Mr. Knoydart," I said; I could never bring myself to call him Whipper Will. In fact, I had never known the Whipper Will who was the terror of trailer parks in four counties. The man I knew, the man before us, was large but soft — beef gone to fat — with no teeth and long, thin white hair (which looked, this morning, a little grayer than usual). His pale blue eyes were fixed on the TV, and his fingers were busy stroking a paper napkin laid across his knee.

"What happened, Daddy?" Candy asked, touching the old man's shoulder tentatively. There was, of course, no answer. Whipper Will Knoydart hadn't spoken to anyone since he had been admitted in January, when he had called the Head Nurse, Florence Gaithers, a "stupid motherfucker, a bitch, and a –––––––," and threatened to shoot her.

"I was helping him out of his wheelchair to go to the bathroom, and he just up and slugged me."

I turned and saw a skinny young black man in whites, standing in the doorway. He wore a diamond stud in his nose and he was dabbing at a black eye with a wet rag.

"He got this look in his eye. Called me a ––––––– (excuse me!), and then he up and hit me. It was almost like the old Whipper Will."

"Sorry, Buzzer. Thanks for calling me instead of Gaithers."

"It's no big deal, Candy. Old folks with Alzheimer's have inci*dents*." Buzzer pronounced it with the accent on the *dent*. "Gaithers would just get all excited."

"Buzzer," said Candy. "I want you to meet —" I was hoping she would introduce me as her soon-to-be-fiancé, but I was disappointed. I was introduced as her "friend from New York."

"Whipper Will's Yank," said Buzzer, nodding. "I heard about him."

"Sorry about your eye," said Candy. "And I do appreciate your not calling Gaithers. Can I buy you a steak to put on it?"

"I'm a vegetarian," said Buzzer. "Don't you worry about it, Candy. Your daddy's not so bad, except for this one incident. He lets me wash him and walk him around every morning just as sweet as anything; don't you, Mister Knoydart? And we watch TNN together. He calls me whenever Pam Tillis comes on, don't you Mr. Knoydart? He wasn't always so sweet, though. Why, I remember one time he took a shot at my mother, when we lived out at Kyber's Creek Trailer Park. Called her a ———. Excuse me, but he did."

"Buzzer and I are old friends," Candy explained as we went back out to the car. "He was the first black kid in my junior high, excuse me, African American, or whatever, and I was Whipper Will's daughter, so we were outcasts together. I looked after him and he's still looking after me. Thank God. If Gaithers finds out Daddy's acting up, she'll kick him out of Squirrel Ridge for sure, and I won't have any place to put him, and we'll be back to square one, and how would that be?"

"Bad," I said.

"Well, hopefully it's over. Just an incident." She said it the same way as Buzzer.

"Hope so," I said.

"Funny thing is, didn't you think Daddy looked better?"

"Better?"

"I think Buzzer's been putting Grecian Formula on his hair. Buzzer always wanted to be a hairdresser. This nursing home thing is just a sideline."

We had managed to miss lunch. We made a date for dinner and "a drive" (tonight was to be my night to pop the question), and Candy dropped me at the office. It was only three o'clock, so I opened a Caffeine-Free Diet Cherry Coke and spread out my *Corcoran's* on the windowsill, determined to make up for lost time. I was awakened by a rhythmic clacking, jacking, cracking, snorting, cavorting noise, and a faint electrical smell. The floor was shaking. Whipper Will's upright fax machine was spitting out a sheet of purple-ink-smeared paper, which drifted to the floor.

I picked it up by one corner and studied it while it cooled:

$$\frac{55}{\Delta} = \left[\frac{H}{32\pi} \quad d \; string(14)\right]^{\frac{1}{4}}_{g^2} > t^{\frac{1}{2}} \int_{0-0}^{0}\infty$$

But before I could figure out what it meant (I knew, of course, who it was from), the phone rang. "There's the answer to your question," Wu said.

"What question?"

"You asked me if something here could already be going backward."

"Not there," I said. "Here."

"By 'here' I mean here on Earth!" Wu said. "And as my calculations show, it is theoretically possible. Perhaps even inevitable. You know about superstrings, right?"

"Sort of like superglue or supermodels?" I ventured.

"Exactly. They hold the Universe together, and they are stretched to the limit. It's *possible* that harmonic vibrations of these superstrings *might* shake loose discrete objects, so that they would appear as bubbles or reversals in local entropic fields."

"Fields? What about vacant lots?" I told Wu about the beaded seat cushion.

"Hmmm," said Wu. I could almost hear his brain whirring. "You *may* be on to something, Irv. Superstring harmonic overtones *could* be backtracking my sightline from the Edge of the Universe, and then following our fax and phone connections. The same way glass breaks along a line when you score it. But we have to be sure. Send me a couple of pictures, so we can *quantify* the — Ooooooops!" His voice dropped to a whisper. "Here comes my boss. Say hi to Candy. I'll call you later."

There was still plenty of afternoon light, so as soon as Wu hung up, I headed across the corner lot to Hoppy's Good Gulf and borrowed the Polaroid he uses to photograph accident scenes. As I took the picture, I *quantified* for myself, by counting. The eleven beads on row four had increased to thirteen, and the other rows also seemed to be much improved. There weren't many beads lying in the dirt. The seat cushion looked almost good enough to put in my car, if I had one.

It was creepy. I didn't like it.

I returned Hoppy's camera and took the long way back to the office, trying to make sense of it all. Were the falling leaves going to float back up and fasten themselves to the trees? Was Candy's Volvo going to have four speeds in reverse? I got so confused just thinking about it that I put the photo into the wicker OUT tray of Whipper Will's upright fax machine before I remembered — I guess *realized* is the word — that I had no outgoing. I could talk to Wu on the phone (when he called me) but I couldn't fax him anything.

Perversely, I was glad. I had done what I could, and now I was tired. Tired of thinking about the Universe. I had an important, indeed a historic, date coming up — not to mention a bar exam to study for. I opened a Caffeine-Free Diet Cherry Coke, spread my *Corcoran's* on the windowsill, and lost myself in pleasant dreams. Mostly of Candy and that last little uniform button.

A Huntsville Parks Department professional has many obligations that run past the normal nine-to-five. Some of them are interesting, some even fun, and since Candy loves her job, I try to accommodate (which means accompany) her whenever possible. That night we had to stop by the North Side Baptist Union Fish Fry and Quilt Show, where Candy was the Guest of Honor in her neatly pressed, knife-creased khakis. The fish was my favorite, pond-raised cat rolled in yellow cornmeal, but I couldn't relax and enjoy myself. I kept thinking of later; I was in a hurry to get up on Squirrel Ridge, the mountain. But one good thing about Baptists, they don't last long, and by nine fifteen Candy and I were parked up at the Overlook. It was a cool night and we sat out on the warm, still-ticking hood of the P1800 with the lights of the valley spread out below us like captured stars. My palms were sweating. This was to be the night I would propose, and hopefully she would accept, with all the privileges that entails.

I wanted the evening to be memorable in every way, and since the Moon was supposed to be full, I waited for it to rise. As I watched the glow on the eastern horizon, I thought of Wu and wondered if the Moon would rise in the west after the "Reversal." Would anyone notice the difference? Or would folks just call the west the east and leave it at that?

It was too deep for me to figure out, and besides — I had other things on my mind. As soon as the Moon cleared the horizon, I got off the hood and dropped to my knees. I was just about to pop the question, when I heard a *beep beep*.

"What's that?" I asked.

"Buzzer," said Candy.

"Sounds like a beeper."

"It is. Buzzer loaned me his beeper," she said, reaching

down to her waist and cutting it off.

"What for?"

"You know what for."

There are no phones up on Squirrel Ridge, so we hightailed it down the mountain with the sus howling and the exhaust barking, alternately. Candy's big fear was alerting Gaithers, who was on duty that night, so we rolled into the parking lot of Squirrel Ridge, the nursing home, with the lights off. I stayed with the P1800 while Candy slipped in through a side door.

She was back in half an hour. "Well?" I prompted.

"Daddy hit Buzzer," she said (or I *thought* she said) as we drove out of the lot as quietly as possible. "It's cool, though. Buzzer didn't say anything to Gaithers. This time. I figure we've got one more strike. Three and we're out."

"Where'd he hit him this time?"

"Not hit," she said. *"Bit."*

"But your daddy doesn't have any teeth!"

Candy shrugged. "Seems he does now."

And that was it for what I had hoped would be one of the biggest evenings of my life. My proposal, with its acceptance, with all the privileges that entails — none of it was to be. Not that night. Candy needed her sleep since she had to leave early in the morning for the annual statewide all-day Parks Department meeting in Montgomery. She dropped me off at Hoppy's Good Gulf and I took a long walk, which is almost as good as a cold shower. It takes only twenty minutes to cover every street in downtown Huntsville. Then I went back to the office, cutting through the corner lot. In the light of the full Moon, the beaded seat cushion looked almost new. The top rows of beads were complete, and there were only a few missing on the lower section. I resisted the urge to kick it.

There were two messages on Whipper Will's ancient reel-to-reel answering machine. The first was just heavy breathing. A random sexual harassment call, I figured. Or a wrong number. Or maybe an old enemy of Whipper Will's; most of Whipper Will's enemies were old.

The second message was from Candy. She had beaten me home. "This is going to be an all-day conference tomorrow," she said. "I won't get home till late. I gave your number to Buzzer, just in case. You know what I mean. When I get home, we'll take care of our *unfinished business*." She signed off with a loud smooching sound. For some reason, I found it depressing.

It was midnight but I couldn't sleep. I kept having these horrible thoughts. I opened a Caffeine-Free Diet Cherry Coke and spread my *Corcoran's* out on the window ledge, overlooking the empty street. Was there ever a downtown as quiet as downtown Huntsville? I tried to imagine what it had looked like before the Bypass had bled away all the business. I must have fallen right to sleep, for I had a nightmare about downtown streets crowded with newlyweds walking hand in hand. And all the newlyweds were old. And all the newlyweds had teeth.

*

The next morning, I woke up thinking about the beaded seat cushion. I decided I needed another picture for Wu, to make it a before-and-after. After my morning ablutions in the Good Gulf men's room, I found Hoppy in the repair bay, fixing the front brakes on yet another Taurus. "Whipper Will's Yank," he said.

"Right," I said. I asked to borrow the Polaroid again.

"It's in the wrecker."

"The wrecker's locked."

"You have the key," Hoppy said. "Your men's room key. One key does everything around here. Keeps life simple. 'Nuff said."

I waited until Hoppy was busy before I took the camera out into the corner lot and photographed the beaded seat cushion. I didn't want him to think I was nuts. I printed the picture and put the camera away, then hurried back to the office and placed the new photo next to the old one in the wicker OUT bin of Whipper Will's ancient upright fax machine. If I had ever doubted my own eyes (and who doesn't, from time to time?), I was convinced now. I had photographic evidence. The beaded seat cushion was in *much* better shape in the second photo than in the first, even though they were less than twenty-four hours apart. It was un-decaying right before my eyes.

I kept having these horrible thoughts.

At least there were no messages on the answering machine. Nothing from Buzzer.

Even though I couldn't concentrate, I knew I needed to

study. I opened a Caffeine-Free Diet Cherry Coke and spread my *Corcoran's* on the windowsill. When I woke up it was almost noon and the floor was shaking; the fax machine was huffing and puffing, creaking and groaning, rattling and whining. It stopped and started again, louder than ever. A sheet of paper fluttered down from the IN bin. I caught it, still warm, before it hit the floor:

$$\lambda = \frac{0.893}{M^{1/3}} \left(\frac{40}{\sqrt{3\frac{1}{m}}} \right) > \frac{3 \times 10^{7}}{\Omega} \Big/ \propto T$$

While I was still trying to decipher it, I realized the phone was ringing.

I picked it up with dread; I whispered, "Buzzer?" assuming the worst.

"Buzzer?" It was Wu. "Are you impersonating a device, Irving? But never mind that, I have a more important question. Which one of these Polaroids is number one?"

"What Polaroids? You *got* them? That's impossible. I never faxed them. I don't have outgoing!"

"Seems you do now," Wu said. "I was faxing you my newest calculations, just now, and as soon as I finished, here came your Polaroids, riding through on the self-checking backspin from the handshake protocol, I guess. You forgot to number them, though."

"The crummy one is number two," I said. "The crummier one is number one."

"So you were right!" Wu said. "It's going from worse to bad. Even in downtown Huntsville, light-years from the Edge, the Universe is already shrinking in isolated anti-entropic bubble fields. Anomalous harmonic superstring overtones. The formula I just faxed through, as I'm sure you can see, confirms the theoretical *possibility* of a linear axis of the Anti-Entropic Reversal Field following a superstring fold from the Edge of the Universe to downtown Huntsville. But observation is the soul of science, and by using your Polaroids, now I will be able to mathematically calculate the…"

"Wu!" I broke in. Sometimes with Wu you have to break in. "What about people?"

"People?"

"People," I said. "You know. Humans. Like ourselves. Bipeds with cars, for Christ's sake!" Sometimes Wu was impossible.

"Oh, *people*," he said. "Well, people are made of the same stuff as the rest of the Universe, aren't they? I mean, *we*. The Anti-Entropic Reversal means that we will live backward, from the grave to the cradle. People will get younger instead of older."

"When?"

"When? When the Anti-Entropic Reversal Wave spreads back, from the Edge through the rest of the Universe. Like the changing tide. Could be several thousand years; could be just a few hundred. Though, as your seat cushion experiment demonstrates, there may be isolated bubbles along the linear axis where… Whoops! Here comes my boss," Wu whispered.

"I have to get off. Give my best to Candy. How's her dad, by the way?"

Wu often signs off with a question, often unanswerable. But this one was more unanswerable than most.

Lunch at the Bonny Bag was strange. I had a whole booth to myself. Plus a lot on my mind.

"Where's Candy?" Bonnie asked.

"Montgomery," I told her.

"The state capital. That lucky dog. And how's Whipper Will? Still sweet as ever?"

"I sure hope so," I said.

"Did I ever tell you about the time he took a shot at my…"

"I think so," I said. I ordered the chicken salad, just for the adventure of it. Plus two bags of chips.

Back at the office, I found two messages on the reel-to-reel answering machine. The first was heavy breathing. The second was ranting and raving. It was all grunts and groans, and I figured it was probably one of Whipper Will's old enemies. The only words I could make out were "motherfucker" and "kill" and "shoot."

Nothing from Buzzer, thank God.

I opened a Caffeine-Free Diet Cherry Coke and spread my *Corcoran's* on the windowsill. I kept having these horrible thoughts, and I knew the only way to get rid of them was to study for the bar. When I woke up it was getting dark. The phone was ringing. I forced myself to pick it up.

"Buzzer... ?" I whispered, expecting the worst.

"Buzzzzzzzzzz!" said Wu, who sometimes enjoys childish humor. But then he got right down to business. "How far apart are these two Polaroids?" he asked.

"In time?" I did some quick figuring. "Eighteen and three-quarter hours."

"Hmmm. That checks out with my rate-of-change figures," he said. "Mathematics is the soul of science, and beads are easier to count than stars. By counting the beads, then subtracting, then dividing by the phase of the Moon over eighteen and three-quarters, I can calculate the exact age of the Universe. Are you on Central or Eastern Standard time?"

"Central," I said. "But Wu..."

"Perfect! If I get a Nobel, remind me to share it with you, Irv. The exact age of the Universe, from the Big Bang until this instant is..."

"Wu!" I broke in. Sometimes with Wu you have to break in. "I need your help. Is there any way to reverse it?"

"Reverse what?"

"The contraction, the Anti-Entropic Reversal, or whatever."

"Turn around the Universe?" He sounded almost offended.

"No, just the little stuff. The anomalous harmonic superstring overtones."

"Hmmm." Wu sounded intrigued again. "Locally? Temporarily? Maybe. If it is all on strings..." I couldn't tell if he was talking about the beaded seat cushion or the Universe.

Whipper Will's upright fax machine grumbled. It rumbled. It growled and it howled. The floor shook and the wall creaked and a warm sheet of paper came out of the IN bin and fluttered toward the floor.

I caught it; I was getting good at catching them:

$$\sqrt{\frac{9}{H}} = \frac{Gd\ ^2R_{jeans}(\pi\cos y)}{\sum 也\ 日'\big]_4 @ \frac{125}{\cos y^3}\sqrt{祐叻竹灬}}\ ^{18b}$$

"What's with the Chinese?" I asked.

"Multicultural synergy," Wu said. "I've combined my calculations of the relative linear stability of the remote Anti-Entropic Fields on the superstring axes, with an ancient Tien Shan spell for precipitating poisons out of a well so that camels can drink. A little trick I picked up in school."

"Medical school?"

"Caravan school," said Wu. "It's temporary, of course. It'll only last a few thousand years. And you'll have to use an Anti-Entropic Field Reversal Device."

"What's that?"

"Whatever's handy. A two-by-four, a jack handle. All it takes is a short sharp shock. The problem is, there's no way to tell what other effects might — Whoooops!" His voice dropped. "Here comes my boss—"

*

After Wu hung up I sat by the window, waiting for night to fall. Waiting for Buzzer to call. I kept having these horrible thoughts.

When it was dark, I walked downstairs and into the corner lot. I carried a short length of two-by-four with me. I squared off and hit the ground beside the beaded seat cushion, just once. A short, sharp shock. Then again, on the other side. Another short, sharp shock. I resisted the urge to destroy it with a kick; it was an experiment, after all.

I tossed the two-by-four into the weeds. The Moon was rising (still in the east) and a dog and a cat were standing side by side on the path, watching me. As they trotted off together, still side by side, a chill gripped my heart: What if I had made things worse?

Hoppy's Good Gulf was closed. I used the men's room and went back to the office. There were two messages on the machine. The first was a voice I had never heard, but I knew exactly who it was. "Where is that vicious pissant daughter of mine? Are you listening to me, bitch? I swore by God if you ever put me in a nursing home I would kill you, and by God I will!"

The second message was from Buzzer. "We've got a problem here, Yank," he said. "The old man is uncontrollable. He threw a chair through a glass door and got into Gaither's office, and now—"

There was a sound of more glass breaking, and a scream, and a thud. I heard a *beep* and I realized that the message was over.

The phone was ringing. I picked it up and heard the first voice again, but this time it was live: "You devil motherfucker bitch bastard! Where is my Oldsmobile? Did you give it to this nursing home nigger?"

I heard Buzzer shout, "No!"

"You fucking -------!"

Then I heard a shot. I hung up the phone and ran out the door, into the night.

When you haven't driven for a while, it can seem almost like a thrill. I wasn't worried about the police; I figured they wouldn't stop Hoppy's Good Gulf wrecker, as long as they didn't notice who was driving. So I turned on the red light and drove like a bat out of Hell out the four-lane toward Squirrel Ridge, the nursing home.

I left the truck in the lot with the engine running and the red light spinning. I found Whipper Will in Gaither's office. He had gotten the gun out of her desk. It was a brand-new, pearl-handled .38, a ladies' special. Whipper Will was holding it on Buzzer, who sat bolt upright behind the desk in one of those rolling office chairs. There was a bullet hole in the wall just to the left of Buzzer's head.

"Take all my money and put me in a God damned nursing home! That rotten little -------!" Whipper Will raved. He was talking about Candy — his own daughter. His hair was almost black and he was standing (I had never seen him standing before) with his back to the door. Buzzer was facing me, making elaborate signals with his eyebrows and diamond nose stud — as if I couldn't figure out the situation on my own! I tiptoed across the floor, trying to avoid crunching the broken glass.

"Wait till I get my hands on that coldhearted, conniving little black-hearted –––––––!"

I had heard enough. I rapped Whipper Will on the side of the head, firmly. A short, sharp shock. He sagged to his knees and I reached around him and took the .38 out of his hand. I was just about to rap him again on the other side of the head, when he slumped all the way down to the linoleum.

"Good going," said Buzzer. "What's that?"

"An Anti-Entropic Field Reversal Device," I said.

"Looks like a flashlight in a tube sock."

"That, too," I said as we dragged Whipper Will, as gently as possible, down the hall toward his room.

It was almost ten o'clock the next morning when I woke up in Whipper Will's office, on the couch I called my bed. I got up and went to the window. There was the wrecker, parked under the sign at Hoppy's Good Gulf, right where I had left it.

I pulled on my pants and went downstairs, across the corner lot. The beaded seat cushion was missing several rows of beads along the top, and at least half of the bottom. Wooden beads were scattered in the red dirt. I stepped carefully, even respectfully, around them.

"Whipper Will's Yank," said Hoppy, who was replacing the front brake pads on yet another Taurus.

"Right," I said.

"How's old Whipper Will?"

"About the same, I hope," I said. I decided there was no point telling Hoppy about borrowing the truck the night before. "You know how it is with old folks."

" 'Nuff said," he said.

When I got back to the office, there were two messages on the machine. The first one was from Buzzer. "Don't worry about Gaithers, Yank," he said. "I told her a story about a burglar, and she won't call the cops because it turns out that the .38 in her desk is illegal. So no problem about that hole in the wall and fingerprints and stuff. I don't see any reason to bother Candy about this incident, do you?"

I didn't. The second message was from Candy. "I'm back. Hope everything went well. See you at the Bonny Bag at twelve."

I opened a Caffeine-Free Diet Cherry Coke and spread out my *Corcoran's* on the windowsill. When I awoke it was almost twelve.

"I had a great trip," Candy said. "Thanks for looking after things. I stopped by Squirrel Ridge on the way into town this morning, and—"

"And?" *And?*

"Daddy looks fine. He was sleeping peacefully in his wheelchair in front of the TV. His hair is almost white again. I think Buzzer washed all that Grecian Formula out of it."

"Good," I said. "It seemed inappropriate to me."

"I feel like things are settled enough," Candy said. She touched the back of my hand. "Maybe we should go up to Squirrel Ridge tonight," she said. "The mountain, not the nursing home. If you know what I mean."

"What'll you two lovebirds have?" Bonnie asked, chalk poised. "How's your Daddy? Ever tell you about the time he took a..."

"You did," I told her. "And we'll have the usual."

If I were making this story up, it would end right here. But in real life, there is always more, and sometimes it can't be left out. That evening on our way out to Squirrel Ridge, the mountain, Candy and I stopped by the nursing home. Whipper Will was sitting quietly in his wheelchair, stroking a napkin, watching Pam Tillis on TNN with Buzzer. The old man's hair was white as snow and I was glad to see there wasn't a tooth in his head. Buzzer gave me a wink and I gave him the same wink back.

That diamond looked damn good.

That night up at the Overlook I got down on my knees and—well, you know (or you can guess) the rest, with all the privileges that entails. That might have been the end of the story except that when I got back to the office the fax was whirring and stuttering and snorting and steaming, and the phone was ringing, too.

I was almost afraid to pick up the phone. What if it was Buzzer again?

But it wasn't. "Congratulations!" Wu said.

I blushed (but I'm an easy blusher). "You heard already?"

"Heard? I can see it! Didn't you get my fax?"

"I'm just now picking it up off the floor."

It was in purple mimeo ink on still-warm paper:

$$H \Big]_0^{\infty} = \Delta \left(\frac{2\pi\ \frac{m}{\varepsilon}}{a\,14\ 8} \right) e \sqrt{\frac{11\ m^2\ \Delta}{+\ \big|\frac{1}{k}\,19 \rangle}}$$

"Must be the Butterfly Effect," Wu said.

Even though butterflies are romantic (in their way), I was beginning to get the idea that Wu wasn't talking about my proposal, and its acceptance, and all the privileges that entails.

"What *are* you talking about?" I asked.

"Chaos and complexity!" Wu said. "A butterfly flaps its wings in the rain forest and causes a snowstorm over Chicago. Linear harmonic feedback. Look at the figures, Irv! Numbers don't lie! You have set up a superstring harmonic wave reversal that has the entire Universe fluttering like a flag in the wind. What did you hit that beaded seat cushion with, anyway?"

"A two-by-four," I said. I didn't see any reason to tell him about Whipper Will.

"Well, you rapped it just right. The red shift is back. The Universe is expanding again. Who knows for how long?"

"I hope until my wedding," I said.

"Wedding?!? You don't mean…"

"I do," I said. "I proposed last night. And Candy accepted. With all the privileges that entails. Will you fly back from Hawaii to be my best man?"

"Sure," Wu said. "Only, it won't be from Hawaii. I'm starting college in San Diego next week."

"San Diego?"

"My work here as a meteorologist is done. Jane and the boys are already in San Diego, where I have a fellowship to study meteorological entomology."

"What's that?"

"Bugs and weather."

"What do bugs have to do with the weather?"

"I just explained it, Irving," Wu said. "I'll send you the figures and you can see for yourself." And he did. But that's a whole other story.

Get Me to the Church on Time

The best way to approach Brooklyn
is from the air. The Brooklyn Bridge
is nice, but let's admit it, to drive (or
bicycle, or worse, walk) into homely old
Brooklyn directly from the shining towers
of downtown Manhattan is to court
deflation, dejection, even depression. The
subway is no better. You ride from one
hole to another: There's no in-between,
no approach, no drama of arrival.

The Kosciusko Bridge over Newtown Creek is okay, because even drab Williamsburg looks lively after the endless, orderly graveyards of Queens. But just as you are beginning to appreciate the tar-paper tenement rooftops of Brooklyn, there she is again, off to the right: the skyline of Manhattan, breaking into the conversation like a tall girl with great hair in a low-cut dress who doesn't have to say a word. It shouldn't be that way, it's not fair, but that's the way it is. No, the great thing about a plane is that you can only see out of one side. I like to sit on the right. The flights from the South come in across the dark wastes of the Pine Barrens, across the shabby, sad little burgs of the Jersey shore, across the mournful, mysterious bay, until the lights of Coney Island loom up out of the night, streaked with empty boulevards. Manhattan is invisible, unseen off to the left, like a chapter in another book or a girl at another party. The turbines throttle back and soon you are angling down across the streetlight-spangled stoops and backyards of my legend-heavy hometown. Brooklyn!

"There it is," I said to Candy.

"Whatever." Candy hates to fly, and she hadn't enjoyed any of the sights, all the way from Huntsville. I tried looking over her. I could see the soggy fens of Jamaica Bay, then colorful, quarrelsome Canarsie, then Prospect Park and Grand Army Plaza; and there was the Williamsburg Tower with its always accurate clock. Amazingly, we were right on time.

I wished now I hadn't given Candy the window seat, but it was our Honeymoon, after all. I figured she would learn to love to fly. "It's beautiful!" I said.

"I'm sure," she muttered.

I was anticipating the usual long holding pattern, which takes you out over Long Island Sound, but before I knew it, we were making one of those heart-stopping wing-dipping jet-plane U-turns over the Bronx, then dropping down over Rikers Island, servos whining and hydraulics groaning as the battered flaps and beat-up landing gear *clunked* into place for the ten thousandth (at least) time. Those PreOwned Air 707s were seasoned travelers, to say the least. The seat belts said Eastern, the pillows said Pan Am, the barf bags said Braniff, and the peanuts said People Express. It all inspired a sort of confidence. I figured if they were going to get unlucky and go down, they would have done so already.

Through the window, the dirty water gave way to dirty concrete, and then the wheels hit the runway with that happy *yelp* so familiar to anyone who has ever watched a movie, even though it's a sound you never actually hear in real life.

And this was real life. New York!

"You can open your eyes," I said, and Candy did, for the first time since the pilot had pushed the throttles forward in Huntsville. I'd even had to feed her over the Appalachians, since she was afraid that if she opened her eyes to see what was on her tray, she might accidentally look out the window. Luckily, dinner was just peanuts and pretzels (a two-course meal).

We were cruising into the terminal like a big, fat bus with wings, when Candy finally looked out the window. She even ventured a smile. The plane was limping a little (flat tire?), but this final part of the flight she actually seemed to enjoy. "At least you didn't hold your breath," I said.

"What?"

"Never mind."

Ding! We were already at the gate, and right on time. I started to grope under the seat in front of me for my shoes. Usually there's plenty of time before everyone starts filing out of the plane, but to my surprise it was already our turn; Candy was pulling at my arm, and impatient-looking passengers, jammed in the aisle behind, were frowning at me.

I carried my shoes out and put them on in the terminal. They're loafers. I'm still a lawyer, even though I don't exactly practice.

"New York, New York," I crooned to Candy as we traversed the tunnel to the baggage pickup. It was her first trip to my hometown; our first trip together anywhere. She had insisted on wearing her Huntsville Parks Department uniform, so that if there was a crash they wouldn't have any trouble ID-ing her body (whoever "they" were), but she would have stood out in the crowd anyway, with her trim good looks.

Not that New Yorkers aren't trim. Or good looking. The black clad, serious-looking people racing by on both sides were a pleasant relief after the Kmart pastels and unremitting sunny smiles of the South. I was glad to be home, even if only for a visit. New Yorkers, so alien and menacing to many, looked welcoming and familiar to me.

In fact, one of them looked *very* familiar...

"Studs!"

It was Arthur "Studs" Blitz from the old neighborhood. Studs and I had been best friends until high school, when we had gone our separate ways. I had gone to Lincoln High in Coney Island, and he had gone to Carousel, the trade school for airline baggage handlers. It looked like he had done well. His green and black baggage handlers uniform was festooned with medals that clinked and clanked as he bent over an access panel under the baggage carousel, changing a battery in a cellular phone. It seemed a funny place for a phone.

"Studs, it's me, Irving. Irv!"

"Irv the Perv!" Studs straightened up, dropping the new battery, which rolled away. I stopped it with my foot while we shook hands, rather awkwardly.

"From the old neighborhood," I explained to Candy as I bent down for the battery and handed it to Studs. It was a 5.211-volt AXR. It seemed a funny battery for a phone. "Studs is one of the original Ditmas Playboys."

"'Playboys'?" Candy was, still is, easily shocked. "'Perv'?"

"There were only two of us," I explained. "We built a tree house."

"A tree house in Brooklyn? But I thought..."

"Everybody thinks that!" I said. "Because of that book."

"What book?"

"Movie, then. But in fact, *lots* of trees grow in Brooklyn. They grow behind the apartments and houses, where people don't see them from the street. Right, Studs?"

Studs nodded, snapping the battery into the phone. "Irv the Perv," he said again.

"Candy is my fiancée. We just flew in from Alabama," I said. "We're on our honeymoon."

"Fiancée? Honeymoon? Alabama?"

Studs seemed distracted. While he got a dial tone and punched in a number, I told him how Candy and I had met (leaving out my trip to the Moon, as told in "The Hole in the Hole"). While he put the phone under the carousel and replaced the access panel, I told him how I had moved to Alabama (leaving out the red-shift and the nursing home, as told in "The Edge of the Universe"). I was just about to explain why we were having the honeymoon before the wedding, when the baggage carousel started up.

"Gotta go," said Studs. He gave me the secret Ditmas Playboy wave and disappeared through an AUTHORIZED ONLY door.

"Nice uniform," said Candy, straightening her own. "And did you see that big gold medallion around his neck? Wasn't that a Nobel Prize?"

"A Nobel Prize for baggage? Not very likely."

Our bags were already coming around the first turn. That seemed like a good sign. "How come there's a cell phone hidden underneath the carousel?" Candy asked, as we picked them up and headed for the door.

"Some special baggage handlers' trick, I guess," I said.

How little, then, I knew!

Flying into New York is like dropping from the twentieth century back into the nineteenth. Everything is crowded, colorful, old — and slow. For example, it usually takes longer to get from LaGuardia to Brooklyn, than from Huntsville to LaGuardia.

Usually! On this, our honeymoon trip, however, Candy and I made it in record time, getting to curbside for the #38 bus just as it was pulling in, and then catching the F train at Roosevelt Avenue just as the doors were closing. No waiting on the curb or the platform; it was hardly like being home! Of course, I wasn't complaining.

After a short walk from the subway, we found Aunt Minnie sitting on the steps of the little Ditmas Avenue row house she and Uncle Mort had bought for seventy-five hundred dollars fifty years ago, right after World War II, smoking a cigarette. She's the only person I know who still smokes Kents.

"You still go outside to smoke?" I asked.

"You know your Uncle Mort," she said. When I was growing up, Aunt Minnie and Uncle Mort had been like second parents, living only a block and a half away. Since my parents had died, they had been my closest relatives. "Plus, it's written into the reverse mortgage — NO SMOKING! They have such rules!"

Born in the Old Country, unlike her little sister, my mother, Aunt Minnie still had the Lifthatvanian way of ending a statement with a sort of verbal shrug. She gave me one of her smokey kisses, and then asked, "So, what brings you back to New York?"

I was shocked. "You didn't get my letters? We're getting married."

Aunt Minnie looked at Candy with new interest. "To an airline pilot?"

"This is Candy!" I said. "She's with the Huntsville Parks Department. You didn't get my messages?"

I helped Candy drag the suitcases inside, and while we had crackers and pickled *lifthat* at the oak table Uncle Mort had built years ago, in his basement workshop, I explained the past six months as best I could. "So you see, we're here on our Honeymoon, Aunt Minnie," I said, and Candy blushed.

"First the honeymoon and then the marriage?!?" Aunt Minnie rolled her eyes toward the mantel over the gas fireplace, where Uncle Mort's ashes were kept. He, at least, seemed unsurprised. The ornate decorative eye on the urn all but winked.

"It's the only way we could manage it," I said. "The caterer couldn't promise the ice sculpture until Thursday, but Candy had to take her days earlier or lose them. Plus, my best man is in South America, or Central America, I forget which, and won't get back until Wednesday."

"Imagine that, Mort," Aunt Minnie said, looking toward the mantel again. "Little Irving is getting married. And he didn't even invite us!"

"Aunt Minnie! You're coming to the wedding. Here's your airline ticket." I slid it across the table toward her and she looked at it with alarm.

"That's a pretty cheap fare."

"PreOwned Air," I said. She looked blank, so I sang the

jingle, *"Our planes are old, but you pocket the gold."*

"You've seen the ads," Candy offered.

"We never watch TV, honey," Aunt Minnie said, patting her hand. "You want us to go to Mississippi? Tonight?"

"Alabama," I said. "And it's not until Wednesday. We have to stay over a Tuesday night to get the midweek nonstop supersaver roundtrip pricebuster honeymoon plus-one fare. The wedding is on Thursday, at noon. That gives us tomorrow to see the sights in New York, which means we should get to bed. Aunt Minnie, didn't you read my letters?"

She pointed toward a stack of unopened mail on the mantel, next to the urn that held Uncle Mort's ashes. "Not really," she said. "Since your Uncle Mort passed on, I have sort of given it up. He made letter openers, you remember?"

Of course I remembered. At my Bar Mitzvah Uncle Mort gave me a letter opener (which irritated my parents, since it was identical to the one they had gotten as a wedding present). He gave me another one for high school graduation. Ditto City College. Uncle Mort encouraged me to go to law school, and gave me a letter opener for graduation. I still have them all, good as new. In fact, they have never been used. It's not like you need a special tool to get an envelope open.

"Aunt Minnie," I said, "I wrote, and when you didn't write back, I called, several times. But you never picked up."

"I must have been out front smoking a cigarette," she said. "You know how your Uncle Mort is about secondhand smoke."

"You could get an answering machine," Candy offered.

"I have one," Aunt Minnie said. "Mort bought it for me at Forty-Seventh Street Photo, right before they went out of business." She pointed to the end table, and sure enough, there was a little black box next to the phone. The red light was blinking.

"You have messages," I said. "See the blinking red light? That's probably me."

"Messages?" she said. "Nobody told me anything about messages. It's an answering machine. I figure it answers the phone, so what's the point in me getting involved?"

"But what if somebody wants to talk to you?" I protested.

She spread her hands; she speaks English but gestures in Lifthatvanian. "Who'd want to talk to a lonely old woman?"

While Aunt Minnie took Candy upstairs and showed her our bedroom, I checked the machine. There were eleven messages, all from me, all telling Aunt Minnie we were coming to New York for our honeymoon, and bringing her back to Alabama with us for the wedding, and asking her, please, to return my call.

I erased them.

Aunt Minnie's guest room was in the back of the house, and from the window I could see the narrow yards where I had played as a kid. It was like looking back on your life from middle age (almost, anyway), and seeing it literally. There were the fences I had climbed, the grapevines I had robbed, the corners I had hidden in. There, two doors down, was Studs's backyard, with the big maple tree. The tree house we had built was still there. I could even see a weird blue light through the cracks. Was someone living in it?

After we unpacked, I took Candy for a walk and showed her the old neighborhood. It looked about the same, but the people were different. The Irish and Italian families had been replaced by Filipinos and Mexicans. Studs's parents' house, two doors down from Aunt Minnie's, was dark except for a light in the basement — and the blue light in the tree house out back. My parents' house, a block and a half away on East Fourth, was now a rooming house for Bangladeshi cab-drivers. The apartments on Ocean Parkway were filled with Russians.

When we got back to the house, Aunt Minnie was on the porch, smoking a Kent. "See how the old neighborhood has gone to pot?" she said. "All these foreigners!"

"Aunt Minnie!" I said, shocked. "You were a foreigner, too, remember? So was Uncle Mort."

"That's different."

"How?"

"Never you mind."

I decided to change the subject. "Guess who I saw at the airport yesterday? Studs Blitz, from down the block, re-member?"

"You mean young Arthur," said Aunt Minnie. "He still lives at home. His father died a couple of years ago. His mother,

Mavis, takes in boarders. Foreigners. Thank God your Uncle Mort's benefits spared me that."

She patted the urn and the cat's eye glowed benevolently.

That night, Candy and I began our Honeymoon by holding hands across the gap between our separate beds. Candy wanted to wait until tomorrow night, after we had "done the tourist thing" to "go all the way." Plus, she was still nervous from the flight.

I didn't mind. It was exciting and romantic. Sort of.

"Your Aunt Minnie is sweet," Candy said, right before we dropped off to sleep. "But can I ask one question?"

"Shoot."

"How can ashes object to smoke?"

Our return tickets were for Wednesday. That meant we had one full Honeymoon day, Tuesday, to see the sights of New York, most of which (all of which, truth be told) are in Manhattan. Candy and I got up early and caught the F train at Ditmas. It came right away. We got off at the next-to-last stop in Manhattan, Fifth Avenue, and walked uptown past St. Patrick's and Tiffany's and Disney and the Trump Tower; all the way to Central Park and the Plaza, that magnet for honeymooners. When we saw all the people on the front step, we thought there had been a fire. But they were just smoking; it was just like Brooklyn.

We strolled through the lobby, peering humbly into the Palm Court and the Oak Room, then started back downtown, still holding hands. Candy was the prettiest girl on Fifth Avenue (one of the few in uniform), and I loved watching her watch my big town rush by. New York! Next stop, Rockefeller Center. We joined the crowd overlooking the skaters, secretly waiting for someone to fall; it's like NASCAR without the noise. Candy was eyeing the line at Nelson's On the Rink, where waiters on Rollerblades serve cappuccinos and lattes. It's strictly a tourist joint; New Yorkers don't go for standing in line and certainly not for coffee. But when I saw how fast the line was moving, I figured, what the Hell. We were seated right away and served right away, and the expense (we are talking four-dollar croissants here) was well worth it.

"What now?" asked Candy, her little rosebud smile deliciously flaked with pastry. I couldn't imagine anyone I would rather honeymoon with.

"The Empire State Building, of course."

Candy grimaced. "I'm afraid of heights."

"We're not going to the top, silly," I said. "That's a tourist thing." Taking her by the hand, I took her on my own personal Empire State Building Tour, which involves circling it and seeing it above and behind and through and between the other midtown buildings; catching it unawares, as it were. We started outside Lord & Taylor on Fifth, then cut west on Fortieth alongside Bryant Park for the sudden glimpse through the rear of a narrow parking lot next to American Standard; then started down Sixth, enjoying the angle from Herald Square (and detouring through Macy's to ride the wooden-treaded escalators). Then we worked back west through "little Korea," catching two dramatic views up open airshafts and one across a steep sequence of fire escapes. Standing alone, the Empire State Building looks stupid, like an oversized toy or a prop for a Superman action figure. But in its milieu it is majestic, like an Everest tantalizingly appearing and disappearing behind the ranges. We circled the great massif in a tightening spiral for almost an hour, winding up (so to speak) on Fifth Avenue again, under the big art deco façade. The curb was crowded with tourists standing in line to buy T-shirts and board buses. The T-shirt vendors were looking gloomy, since the buses were coming right away and there was no waiting.

I had saved the best view for last. It's from the middle of Fifth Avenue, looking straight up. You have to time it just right with the stoplights, of course. Candy and I were about to step off the curb, hand in hand, when a messenger in yellow-and-black tights (one of our city's colorful jesters), who was straddling his bike beside a rack of pay phones on the corner of Thirty-Third, hailed me.

"Yo!"

I stopped. That's how long I'd been in Alabama.

"Your name Irv?"

I nodded. That's how long I'd been in Alabama.

He handed me the phone with a sort of a wink and a sort of a shrug, and was off on his bike before I could hand it back (which was my first instinct).

I put the phone to my ear. Rather cautiously, as you might imagine. "Hello?"

"Irv? Finally!"

"Wu?!?" Everybody should have a friend like Wilson Wu, my best man. Wu studied physics at Bronx Science, pastry in Paris, math at Princeton, herbs in Taiwan, law at Harvard (or was it Yale?), and caravans at a Gobi caravansary. Did I mention he's Chinese-American, can tune a twelve string guitar in under a minute with a logarithmic calculator, and is over six feet tall? I met him when we worked at Legal Aid, drove Volvos, and went to the Moon; but that's another story. Then he went to Hawaii and found the Edge of the Universe, yet another story still. Now he was working as a meteorological entomologist, whatever that was, in the jungles of Quetzalcan.

Wherever that was.

"Who'd you expect?" Wu asked. "I'm glad you finally picked up. Your Aunt Minnie told me you and Candy were in midtown doing the tourist thing."

"We're on our honeymoon."

"Oh no! Don't tell me I missed the wedding!"

"Of course not," I said. "We had to take the honeymoon first so Candy could get the personal time. How'd you persuade Aunt Minnie to answer the phone? Or me, for that matter? Are you in Huntsville already?"

"That's the problem, Irv. I'm still in Quetzalcan. The rain forest, or to be more precise, the cloud forest; the canopy, in fact. Camp Canopy, we call it."

"But the wedding is Thursday! You're the best man, Wu! I've already rented your tux. It's waiting for you at Five Points Formal Wear."

"I know all that," said Wu. "But I'm having a problem getting away. That's why I called, to see if you can put the wedding off for a week."

"A week? Wu, that's impossible. Cindy has already commissioned the ice sculpture."

Wu's wife, Cindy, was catering the wedding.

"The hurricane season is almost upon us," said Wu, "and my figures are coming out wrong. I need more time."

"What do the hurricanes have to do with your figure?" I asked. "Or with meteors or bugs, for that matter?"

"Irving — " Wu always called me by my full name when he was explaining something he felt he shouldn't have to explain. "Meteorology is *weather*, not meteors. And the bugs have to do with the Butterfly Effect. We've been over this before."

"Oh yes, of course, I remember," I said, and I did, sort of. But Wu went over it again anyway: how the flap of a butterfly's wing in the rain forest could cause a storm two thousand miles away. "It was only a matter of time," he said, "before someone located that patch of rain forest, which is where we are, and cloned the butterfly. It's a moth, actually. We have twenty-two of them, enough for the entire hurricane season. We can't stop the hurricanes, but we can delay, direct, and divert them a little, which is why ABC flew us down here."

"ABC?"

"They bought the television rights to the hurricane season, Irv. Don't you read the trades? CBS got the NBA and NBC got the Super Bowl. ABC beat out Ted Turner, which is fine with me. Who needs a Hurricane Jane, even upgraded from a tropical storm? The network hired us to edge the 'canes toward the weekends as much as possible, when the news is slow. And State Farm is chipping in, since any damage we can moderate is money in their pocket. They are footing the bill for this little Hanging Hilton, in fact. 'Footing,' so to speak. My feet haven't touched the ground in three weeks."

"I built a tree house once," I said. "Me and Studs Blitz, back in the old neighborhood."

"A tree house in Brooklyn?" interjected a strangely accented voice.

"Who's that?" I asked.

"Dmitri, stay off the line!" barked Wu. "I'll explain later," he said to me. "But I'm losing my signal. Which way are you two lovebirds heading?"

We were heading downtown. Our first stop was Sweet Nothings, the bridal boutique in New York's historic lingerie district. Candy made me wait outside while she shopped. Inspired, I bought a Honeymoon Bungee at the Oriental Novelty Arcade on Broadway. ("What's it for?" Candy asked apprehensively. I promised to show her later.) Feeling romantic, I took her little hand in mine and led her back over to Sixth Avenue and presented her with the world's largest interactive bouquet—a three-block stroll through the flower market. We were just emerging from a tunnel of flowering ferns at Twenty-Sixth, when the pay phone on the corner rang. On a hunch, I picked it up.

When you get hunches as rarely as I do, you follow them.

"Irving, why do you take so long to answer?"

"I picked up on the first ring, Wu. How'd you manage that phone thing, anyway?"

"Software," Wu said. "I swiped the algos for handwriting recognition out of an Apple Newton and interlaced them into a GPS (Global Positioning System) satellite feed program. Then I ran your mail order consumer profile (pirated from J. Crew) through a fuzzilogical bulk mail collator macro lifted off a ZIP code CD-ROM, and adjusted for the fact that you've spent the past six months in Alabama. A friend in the *Mir* shunts the search feeds through the communications satellite LAN until the 'IRV' probability field collapses and the phone nearest you rings. And you pick it up. Voilà!"

"I don't mean that," I said. "I mean, how'd you get Aunt Minnie to answer the phone?"

"I changed the ring!" Wu said, sounding pleased with himself. "It took a little doing, but I was able to tweak a caller ID macro enough to toggle her ringer. Made it sound like a doorbell chime. Somehow that gets her to answer. I'll send you the figures."

"Never mind," I said. "The only figure I want to see is you-know-who's in her Sweet Nothings" (Candy, who was pretending not to listen, blushed) "and yours in a white tux at noon on Thursday! There's no way we can change the wedding date."

"Can't you put it off at least a couple of days, Irv? I'm having trouble with my formula."

"Impossible!" I said. "The ice sculpture won't wait. Let the butterflies go and get on back to Huntsville. One hurricane more or less can't make all that much difference."

"Moths," said Wu. "And it's not just hurricanes. What if it rains on your wedding?"

"It won't," I said. "It can't. Cindy guarantees clear skies. It's included in the catering bill."

"Of course it is, but how do you think that works, Irving? Cindy buys weather insurance from Ido Ido, the Japanese wedding conglomerate, which contracts with Entomological Meteorological Solutions — that's us — to schedule outdoor ceremonies around the world. It's just a sideline for EMS, of course. A little tweaking. But I can't release the first moth until the coordinates are right, and my numbers are coming out slippery."

"Slippery?"

"The math doesn't work, Irv. The Time axis doesn't line up. In a system as chaotic as weather, you only have one constant, Time, and when it isn't..."

But we were losing our signal, and Candy was looking at me suspiciously. I hung up.

"What are all these phone calls from Wu?" she asked, as we headed downtown. "Is something wrong with the wedding plans?"

"Absolutely not," I lied. There was no reason to spoil her honeymoon (and mine!). "He just wants me to help him with a — a math problem."

"I thought he was the math whiz. I didn't know you even took math."

I didn't, not after my sophomore year in high school. I was totally absorbed by history, inspired by my favorite teacher, Citizen Tipograph (she wanted us to call her Comrade, but the principal put his foot down), who took us on field trips as far afield as Gettysburg and Harpers Ferry. Every course C.T. taught, whether it was Women's Labor History, Black Labor History, Jewish Labor History, or just plain old American Labor History, included at least one trip to Union Square, and I grew to love the seedy old park, where I can still hear the clatter of the horses and the cries of the Cossacks (which is what C.T. called the cops) and the stirring strains of the *Internationale*. I tried to share some of this drama with Candy, but even though she listened politely, I could see that to her Union Square was just scrawny grass, dozing bums, and overweening squirrels.

Candy couldn't wait to get out of the park. She was far more interested in the stacked TVs in the display window at Nutty Ned's Home Electronics, on the corner of University and Fourteenth, where dozens of Rosie O'Donnells were chatting silently with science fiction writer Paul Park. There's nothing better than a talk show without sound. We both stopped to watch for a moment, when all of the screens started scrolling numbers. Over Rosie and her guest!

On a hunch, I went into the store. Candy followed.

Nutty Ned's clerks were firing wildly with remotes, trying to tune the runaway TVs. The displays all changed colors but stayed the same. It was strange, but strangely familiar:

$$\frac{\frac{W}{M}\ |\psi\rangle}{UHF}_{.21\,cm} = \frac{w(x,t)}{3.2\,\text{Imb}}\sum_{l=1}^{k} \frac{\left(\xi(\theta>0)\right)}{\frac{1372}{(63C_2)\Delta}}^{\phi(x')}$$

I figured I knew what it was. And I was right. At precisely that moment, an entire FINAL SALE table of cordless phones started to ring. It made a terrible noise, like a nursery filled with children who decide to cry all at once.

I picked up one and they all quit.

"Wu? Is that you?"

"Irv, did you see my figures? I'm shunting them through the midmorning talk net COMSAT feed. See what I mean? I'm getting totally unlikely dates and places for these hurricanes, all down the line. Not to mention rainy weddings. And it's definitely the T."

"The T?"

"The Time axis, the constant that makes the Butterfly

Effect predictable. It's become a maverick variable, too long here, too short there. Speaking of which, I wish you wouldn't make me ring you twenty times. It's annoying, and I have other things to do here, living in a tree house, like feed the flying—"

"I picked up on the first ring."

"The heck you did! The phone rang twenty-six times."

I did a quick count of the phones on the FINAL SALE table. "Twenty-six phones rang, Wu, but they each rang only once. And all at once."

"Whoa!" said Wu. "I'm coming through in parallel? That could mean there's a twist."

"A twist?"

"A twist in local space-time. It's never happened but it's theoretically possible, of course. And it just *might* explain my slippery T-axis. Have you noticed any other temporal anomalies?"

"Temporary comedies?"

"Weird time stuff, Irving! Any other weird time stuff happening there in New York? Overturned schedules? Unexpected delays?"

"Well, New York's all about delays," I said, "but as a matter of fact—" I told Wu about never having to wait for the subway. Or the bus. "Even the Fifth Avenue bus comes right away!"

"The Fifth Avenue bus! I'm beginning to think there may be more than a temporal anomaly here. We may be looking at a full-fledged chronological singularity. But I need more than your subjective impressions, Irv; I need hard numbers.

Which way are you two lovebirds going?"

"Downtown," I said. "It's almost lunchtime."

"Perfect!" he said. "How about Carlo's?"

When Wu and I had worked at Legal Aid, on Centre Street, we had often eaten at Carlo's Calamari in Little Italy. But only when we had time to take a *loooong* lunch.

"No way!" I said. "It takes forever to get waited on at Carlo's."

"Exactly!" said Wu.

I felt a tap on my shoulder. "You plan to buy this phone?" It was Nutty Ned himself. I recognized his nose from the TV ads.

"No way," I said.

"Then hang it the fuck up, please."

"We got a menu as soon as we sat down," I said. I was speaking on the model Camaro phone at Carlo's, while Candy poked through her cold seafood salad, setting aside everything that had legs or arms or eyes, which was most of the dish.

"Impossible!" said Wu.

"We ordered and my primavera pesto pasta came right away. Maybe they have it already cooked and they just microwave it." I said this low so the waiter wouldn't hear. He had brought me the phone on a tray shaped like Sicily. It was beige, flecked with red. Dried blood? Carlo's is a mob joint. Allegedly.

"What's right away?"

"I don't know, Wu. I didn't time it."

"I need numbers, Irv! What about breadsticks? Do they still have those skinny hard breadsticks? How many did you eat between the time you ordered and the time the food came?"

"Three."

"Three apiece?"

"Three between us. Does knowing that really help?"

"Sure. I can use it either as one and one-half, or as three over two. Numbers don't lie, Irv. Parallel or serial, I'm beginning to think my T-axis problem is centered in New York. Everything there seems to be speeded up slightly. Compressed."

"Compressed," I said. When Wu is talking he expects you to respond. I always try and pick a fairly innocuous word and just repeat it.

"You've got it, Irv. It's like those interviews on TV that are a little jumpy, because they edit out all the connective time — the uhs, the ahs, the waits, the pauses. Something's happened to the connective time in New York. That's why the phone rings ten times for me here — actually an average of 8.411 — and only once for you."

"How can the phone ring more times for you than for me?"

"Ever heard of Relativity, Irving?"

"Yes, but…"

"No buts about it!" Wu said. "Theoretically, a ninety-degree twist could cause a leakage of connective time. But what is causing the twist? That's the…"

His voice was starting to fade. Truthfully, I was glad. I was ready to concentrate on my primavera pesto pasta.

"Pepper?" asked the waiter.

"Absolutely," I said. I don't really care for pepper, but I admire the way they operate those big wrist-powered wooden machines.

Candy loves to shop (who doesn't?) so we headed across Grand Street to Soho, looking for jeans on lower Broadway. Since there was no waiting for the dressing rooms (maybe Wu was on to something!), Candy decided to try on one pair of each brand in each style and each color. We were about a third of the way through the stack, when the salesgirl began to beep; rather, her beeper did.

"Your name Irv?" she asked, studying the readout. "You can use the sales phone." It was under the counter, by the shopping bags.

"How's the coffee?" Wu asked.

"Coffee?"

"Aren't you at Dean and DeLuca?"

"We're at ZigZag Jeans."

"On Broadway at Grand? Now my fuzzilogical GPS transponder is showing slack!" Wu protested. "If I'm three blocks off already, then that means…"

I stopped listening. Candy had just stepped out of the dressing room to check her Levis in the store's "rear view" mirror. "What do you think?" she asked.

"Incredible," I said.

"My reaction exactly," said Wu. "But what else could it be? The bus, the breadsticks, the F train — all the numbers seem to indicate a slow leak of connective time somewhere in the New York metropolitan area. Let me ask you this, was your plane on time?"

"Why, yes," I said. "At the gate, as a matter of fact. The little bell went *ding* and everybody stood up at 7:32. I remember noticing it on my watch. It was our exact arrival time."

"Seven thirty-two," repeated Wu. "That helps. I'm going to check the airports. I can patch into their security terminals and interlace from there to the arrival and departure monitors. I'll need a little help, though. Dmitri, are you there? He's sulking."

"Whatever," I said, giving the ZigZag girls back their phone. Candy was trying on the Wranglers, and me, I was falling in love all over again. I rarely see her out of her uniform, and it is a magnificent sight.

In the end, so to speak, it was hard to decide. The Levis, the Lees, the Wranglers, the Guess Whos, the Calvins, and the Glorias all cosseted and caressed the same incredible curves. Candy decided to buy one pair of each and put them all on my credit card, since hers was maxed out. By the time the ZigZag girls had the jeans folded and wrapped and packed up in shopping bags, it was 3:30 — almost time to head back to Brooklyn if we wanted to beat the rush hour. But Wu had given me an idea.

Even guys like me, who can't afford the Israeli cantaloupes

or free-range Pyrenees sheep cheese at Dean and DeLuca, can spring for a cup of coffee, which you pick up at a marble counter between the vegetable and bread sections, and drink standing at tall, skinny chrome tables overlooking the rigorously fashionable intersection of Broadway and Prince.

D&D is my idea of class, and it seemed to appeal to Candy as well, who was back in uniform and eliciting (as usual) many an admiring glance both on the street and in the aisles. I wasn't halfway through my Americano before the butcher appeared from the back of the store with a long, skinny roll of what I thought at first was miniature butcher paper (unborn lamb chops?), but was in fact thermal paper from the old-fashioned adding machine in the meat department. The key to Dean and DeLuca's snooty charm is that everything (except, of course, the customers) is slightly old-fashioned. Hence, thermal paper.

"You Irv?"

I nodded.

He handed me the little scroll. I unrolled it enough to see that it was covered with tiny figures, then let it roll back up again.

"From Wu?" Candy asked.

"Probably," I said. "But let's finish our coffee."

At that very moment, a man walking down Broadway took a cellular phone out of his Armani suit, unfolded it, put it to his ear, and stopped. He looked up and down the street, then in the window at me.

I nodded, somewhat reluctantly. It would have been rude,

even presumptuous, to expect him to bring the phone inside the store to me, so I excused myself and went out to the street.

"Did you get my fax?" asked Wu.

"Sort of," I said. I made a spinning motion with one finger to Candy, who understood right away. She unrolled the little scroll of thermal paper and held it up to the window glass:

$$LGA \, \| = \cancel{\phi} \qquad \qquad \begin{array}{l} \phi \, ieC \\ \text{ONTIME} \\ \text{ONTIME} \\ \text{ON TIME} \end{array} \quad (1300)$$

$$3^3 \qquad \overline{137 > 87} \quad \Sigma$$

$$\phi \quad V \qquad \qquad 12 \, \phi$$

$$\phi \qquad t = 0$$

$$\overline{(\{ \partial h > 8 >> 125.4))}$$

"Well?"

"Well!" I replied. That usually satisfied Wu, but I could tell he wanted more this time. Sometimes with Wu it helps to ask a question, if you can think of an intelligent one. "What's the ON TIME ON TIME ON TIME stuff?" I asked.

"Those are airport figures, Irv! LaGuardia, to be specific. All the planes are on time! That tell you something?"

"The leak is at LaGuardia?" I ventured.

"Exactly! Numbers don't lie, Irv, and as those calculations clearly show, the connective temporal displacement at LaGuardia is exactly equal to the Time axis twist I'm getting worldwide, adjusted for the Earth's rotation, divided by 5.211. Which is the part I can't figure."

"I've seen that number somewhere before," I said. I dimly remembered something rolling around. "A shoe size? A phone number?"

"Try to remember," said Wu. "That number might lead us to the leak. We know it's somewhere at LaGuardia; now all we have to do is pinpoint it. And plug it."

"Why plug it?" I said. "This no-delay business just makes life better. Who wants to wait around an airport?"

"Think about it, Irving!" Wu said. There was an edge to his voice, like when he thinks I am being stupid on purpose. In fact I am never stupid on purpose. That would be stupid. "You know how a low-pressure area sucks air from other areas? It's the same with Time. The system is trying to stabilize itself. Which is why I can't get the proper EMS figures for Hurricane Relief, or Ido Ido, for that matter. Which is why I asked you to delay your wedding in the first place."

"Okay, okay," I said. I was so excited about my upcoming honeymoon that I had totally forgotten the wedding. "So let's plug it. What do you want me to do?"

"Go to LaGuardia and wait for my call," he said.

"LaGuardia?!? Aunt Minnie is expecting us for supper."

"I thought she was Lifthatvanian. They can't cook!"

"They can so!" I said. "Besides, we're sending out for pizza. And besides —" I dropped my voice, " — tonight's the night

Candy and I officially have our honeymoon."

Honeymoon is one of those words you can't say without miming a kiss. Candy must have been reading my lips through Dean & DeLuca's window, because she blushed; beautifully, I might add.

But Wu must not have heard me, because he was saying, "As soon as you get to LaGuardia..." as his voice faded away. We were losing our connection.

Meanwhile, the guy whose phone it was, was looking at his watch. It was a Movado. I recognized it from the *New Yorker* ads. I kept my subscription even after moving to Huntsville. I gave him his phone back and we headed for the subway station.

How could Wu expect me to hang out at LaGuardia waiting for his call on the night of my honeymoon? Perhaps if the Queens-bound train had come first, I might have taken it, but I don't think so. And it didn't. Taking Candy by the hand, I put us on the Brooklyn-bound F. It wasn't quite rush hour, which meant we got a seat as soon as we reached Delancey Street. Did I mention that the train came right away?

Even though (or perhaps because) I am a born and bred New Yorker, I get a little nervous when the train stops in the tunnel under the East River. This one started and stopped, started and stopped.

Then stopped.

The lights went out.

They came back on.

"There is a grumbashievous willin brashabrashengobrak our signal," said the loudspeaker. "Please wooshagranny the delay."

"What did she say?" asked Candy. "Is something wrong?"

"Don't worry about it," I said.

Turned out we were in the conductor's car. The lights flickered but stayed on, and she stepped out of her tiny compartment, holding a phone. "Ashabroshabikus Irving?" she asked.

I nodded.

"Frezzhogristis quick," she said, handing me the phone.

"Hello?" I ventured. I knew who it was, of course.

"Irv, I need you in baggage claim," said Wu.

"In what?"

"I'm closing in on the connective time leak. I think it's a phone somewhere on the Baggage Claim and Ground Transportation level. I need you to go down there and see which payphone is off the hook, so we can... What's that noise?"

"That's the train starting up again," I said.

"Train? I thought you were at the airport."

"I tried to tell you, Wu," I said. "We promised Aunt Minnie we would come home for dinner. Plus, tonight's my honeymoon. Plus, you're not looking for a pay phone."

"How do you know?"

"The 5.211. Now I remember what it was. It was a battery for a cell phone. It was rolling and I stopped it with my foot."

"Of course!" said Wu. "What a fool I am! And you, Irv, are a genius! Don't make a move until I..."

But we were losing our signal.

"Make if sharanka bresh?" asked the conductor, a little testily. She took her phone and stepped back into her tiny compartment and closed the door.

Every bad pizza is bad in its own way, but good pizza is all alike. Bruno's on the corner of Ditmas and MacDonald, under the el, is my favorite, and Aunt Minnie's too. A fresh pie was being popped into the oven as Candy and I walked in the door, and Bruno, Jr., assured us it was ours.

We were headed for home, box in hand, when a battered Buick gypsy cab pulled up at the curb. I waved it off, shaking my head, figuring the driver thought we'd flagged him down. But that wasn't it.

The driver powered down his window and I heard Wu's voice over the static on the two-way radio: "Irv, you can head for Brooklyn after all. I found it. Irv, you there?"

The driver was saying something in Egyptian and trying to hand me his radio mike. I gave Candy the pizza to hold, and took it.

"Press the little button," said Wu.

I pressed the little button. "Found what?"

"The leak. The 5.211 was the clue," said Wu. "I should have recognized it immediately as a special two-year cadmium silicone battery for a low-frequency, high-intensity, short-circuit, long-distance cellular phone. Once you tipped me off, I located the phone hidden underneath the old Eastern/Braniff/Pan Am/Piedmont/People baggage carousel."

"I know," I said, pressing the little button. "I saw it there. So now I guess you want me to go to LaGuardia and hang it up?"

"Not so fast, Irv! The phone is just the conduit, the time-line through which the connective time is being drained. What we need to find is the number the phone is calling — the source of the leak, the actual hole in Time, the twist. It could be some bizarre natural singularity, like a chronological whirlpool or tornado; or even worse, some incredibly advanced, diabolical machine, designed to twist a hole in space-time and pinch off a piece of our Universe. The open phone connection will lead us to it, whatever it is, and guess what?"

"What?"

"The number it's calling is in Brooklyn, and guess what?"

"What?"

"It's the phone number of Dr. Radio Dgjerm!"

He pronounced it rah-dio. I said, "Help me out."

"The world-famous Lifthatvanian resort developer, Irving!" said Wu, impatiently. "Winner of the Nobel Prize for Real Estate in 1982! Remember?"

"Oh, him. Sort of," I lied.

"Which was later revoked when he was indicted for trying to create an illegal universe, but that's another story. And guess what?"

"What?"

"He lives somewhere on Ditmas, near your aunt, as a matter of fact. We're still trying to pinpoint the exact address."

"What a coincidence," I said. "We're on Ditmas right now. We just picked up a pizza."

"With what?"

"Mushrooms and peppers on one side, for Aunt Minnie. Olives and sausage on the other, for Candy. I pick at both, since I like mushrooms and sausage."

"What a coincidence," said Wu. "I like it with olives and peppers." He sighed. "I would kill for a hot pizza. Ever spend six weeks in a tree house?"

"Ever spend six months in a space station?" asked a strangely accented voice.

"Butt out, Dmitri," Wu said (rather rudely, I thought). "Aren't you supposed to be looking for that address?"

"I spent three nights in a tree house once," I said. "Me and Studs. Of course, we had a TV."

"A TV in a tree house?"

"Just black and white. It was an old six-inch Dumont from my Uncle Mort's basement."

"A six-inch Dumont!" said Wu. "Of course! What a fool I am! Irv, did it have…"

But we were losing our signal. Literally. The driver of the gypsy cab was leaning out of his window, shouting in Egyptian and reaching for his microphone.

"Probably has a fare to pick up," I explained to Candy as he snatched the little mike out of my hand and drove off, burning rubber. "Let's get this pizza to Aunt Minnie before it gets cold. Otherwise she'll cook. And she can't."

*

Different cultures deal with death, dying, and the dead in different ways. I was accustomed to Aunt Minnie's Lifthatvanian eccentricities, but I was concerned about how Candy would take it when she set Uncle Mort's ashes at the head of the table for dinner.

Candy was cool, though. As soon as supper was finished, she helped Aunt Minnie with the dishes (not much of a job), and joined her on the front porch for her Kent. And, I supposed, girl talk. I took the opportunity to go upstairs and strap the legs of the twin beds together with the $1.99 Honeymoon Bungee I had bought in Little Korea. The big evening was almost upon us! There on the dresser was the sleek little package from Sweet Nothings: Candy's honeymoon negligee. I was tempted to look inside, but of course I didn't.

I wanted to be surprised. I wanted everything to be perfect.

From the upstairs window I could see the big maple tree in Studs's backyard. It was getting dark, and blue light spilled out through every crack in the tree house, of which there were many.

I heard the doorbell chime. That seemed strange, since I knew Candy and Aunt Minnie were on the front porch. Then I realized it was the phone. I ran downstairs to pick it up.

"Diagonal, right?"

"What?"

"The screen, Irving! On the Dumont you had in the tree house. You said it was a six-inch. Was that measured diagonally?"

"Of course," I said. "It's always measured diagonally. Wu, what's this about?"

"Blonde cabinet?"

"Nice blonde veneer," I said. "The color of a Dreamsicle™. It was a real old set. It was the first one Aunt Minnie and Uncle Mort had bought back in the fifties. It even had little doors you could close when you weren't watching it. I always thought the little doors were to keep the cowboys from getting out when it was turned off."

"Cowboys in Brooklyn?" asked a strangely accented voice.

"Butt out, Dmitri," Wu said. "Irv, you are a genius. We have found the twist."

"I am? We have?"

"Indubitably. Remember the big Dumont console payola recall scandal of 1957?"

"Not exactly. I wasn't born yet. Neither were you."

"Well, it wasn't *really* about payola at all. It was about something far more significant. Quantum physics. Turns out that the #515-gauge boson rectifier under the 354V67 vacuum tube in the Dumont six-inch console had a frequency modulation that set up an interference wave of 8.48756 gauss, which, when hooked up to household 110, opened an oscillating 88-degree offset permeability in the fabric of the space-time continuum."

"A twist?"

"Exactly. And close enough to ninety degrees to make a small leak. It was discovered, quite by accident, by a lowly assistant at Underwriters Laboratory eleven months after the sets had been on the market. Shipped. Sold."

"I don't remember ever hearing about it."

"How could you? It was covered up by the powers-that-be; rather, that-were; indeed, that-still-are. Can you imagine the panic if over a quarter of a million people discovered that the TV set in their living room was pinching a hole in the Universe? Even a tiny one? It would have destroyed the industry in its infancy. You better believe it was hushed up, Irv. Deep-sixed. Three hundred thirty-seven thousand, eight hundred seventy-seven sets were recalled and destroyed, their blonde wood cabinets broken up for kindling, their circuits melted down for new pennies, and their #515-gauge boson rectifiers sealed in glass and buried in an abandoned salt mine twelve hundred feet under East Gramling, West Virginia."

"So what are you saying? One got away?"

"Exactly, Irv. Three hundred thirty-seven thousand, eight hundred seventy-*seven* were destroyed, but three hundred thirty-seven thousand, eight hundred seventy *eight* were manufactured. Numbers don't lie. Do the math."

"Hmmm," I said. "Could be that Aunt Minnie missed the recall. She hardly ever opens her mail, you know. Studs and I found the set in Uncle Mort's basement workshop. It hadn't been used for years, but it seemed to work okay. We didn't notice it twisting any hole in Time."

"Of course not. It's a tiny hole. But over a long period, it would have a cumulative effect. Precisely the effect we are seeing, in fact. Many millions of connective milliseconds have been drained out of our Universe — perhaps even stolen deliberately, for all we know."

I was relieved. If it was a crime, I was off the hook. I could concentrate on my honeymoon. "Then let's call the police," I said.

Wu just laughed. "The police aren't prepared to deal with anything like this, Irv. This is quantum physics, Feynman stuff, way beyond them. We will have to handle it ourselves. When Dmitri finds the address for Dr. Dgjerm, I have a suspicion we will also find out what became of the legendary Lost D6."

"Isn't this a bit of a coincidence?" I asked. "What are the odds that the very thing that is messing you up in Quetzalcan is right here in my old neighborhood in Brooklyn? It seems unlikely."

"That's because you don't understand probability, Irving," said Wu. "Everything is unlikely until it happens. Look at it this way: When there's a ten percent chance of rain, there's a ninety percent chance it won't rain, right?"

"Right."

"Then what if it starts raining? The probability wave collapses, and the ten percent becomes a hundred, the ninety becomes zero. An unlikely event becomes a certainty."

It made sense to me. "Then it's raining here, Wu," I said. "The probability waves are collapsing like crazy, because the TV you are looking for is still in the tree house. Turned on, in fact. I can see the blue light from here. It's in the maple tree in Studs's backyard, three doors down."

"On Ditmas?"

"On Ditmas."

"So your friend Studs could be involved?"

"That's what I was trying to tell you!" I said. "He runs the baggage carousel at LaGuardia that the phone was hidden under."

"The plot thickens," said Wu, who loves it when the plot thickens. "He must be draining off the connective time to speed up his baggage delivery! But where is it going? And what is Dgjerm's role in this caper? We'll know soon enough."

"We will?"

"When you confront them, Irv, at the scene of the crime, so to speak. You said it was only three doors away."

"No way," I said. "Not tonight."

"Why not?"

"Guess who?" I felt hands over my eyes.

"Candy, that's why," I said.

"Right you are!" Candy said. Her voice dropped to a whisper: "Coming upstairs?"

"You mean your honeymoon?" Wu asked.

"Yes, of course I mean my honeymoon!" I said, as I watched Candy kiss Aunt Minnie goodnight and go upstairs. "I don't want to confront anybody! Any guys, anyway. Can't you just turn the TV off by remote?"

"There's no remote on those old Dumonts, Irv. You're going to have to unplug it."

"Tomorrow, then."

"Tonight," said Wu. "It'll only take you a few minutes. If the leak is plugged tonight I can redo my calculations and release the first moth in the morning. Then if I catch the nonstop from Quetzalcan City, I'll make Huntsville in time to pick up my tux. But if I don't, you won't have a best man. Or a ring. Or maybe even a wedding. Don't forget, this moth works for Ido Ido, too. What if it rains?"

"Okay, okay," I said. "You convinced me. But I'm just going to run over there and unplug it and that's all." I kissed Aunt Minnie goodnight (she sleeps in the Barcalounger in front of the TV with Uncle Mort's ashes in her lap), then called up the stairs to Candy, "Be up in a minute!"

Then headed out the back door.

I'll never forget the first time I visited my cousin Lucy in New Jersey. Lots of things in the suburbs were different. The trees were skinnier, the houses were lower, the cars were newer, the streets were wider, the yards were bigger, and the grass was definitely greener. But the main thing I remember was my feeling of panic: There was nowhere to hide! The picture windows, one on each house, seemed to stare out onto a world in which nobody had anything to conceal, a terrifying idea to a preteen (I was eleven going on fifteen) since adolescence is the slow, unfolding triumph of experience over innocence, and teens have everything to hide.

I was glad to get back to Brooklyn, where everyone knew who I was but no one was watching me. I had the same safe feeling when I slipped out the kitchen door into Aunt Minnie's tiny (and sadly neglected) backyard. The yards in Brooklyn, on Ditmas at least, are narrow slivers separated by board fences, wire fences, slat fences, mesh fences. Adulthood in America doesn't involve a lot of fence climbing, and I felt like a kid again as I hauled myself carefully over a sagging section of chain-link into the Murphys' yard next door. Of course, they weren't the Murphys anymore: They were the Wing-Tang somethings, and they had replaced the old squealing swing set with a new plastic and rubberoid play center in the shape of a pirate ship, complete with plank.

The next yard, the Patellis', was even less familiar. It had always been choked with flowers and weeds in a dizzying, improbable mix, under a grape arbor that, properly processed, kept the grandfather mildly potted all year. The vines had stopped bearing when "Don Patelli" had died the year I started high school. "Grapes are like dogs," Uncle Mort had said. "Faithful to the end." Everything Uncle Mort knew about dogs, he had learned from books.

A light came on in the house, and I remembered with alarm that the Patellis no longer lived there, and that I was no longer a neighborhood kid; or even a kid. If anybody saw me, they would call the police. I stepped back into the shadows. Looking up, and back a house or two, I spotted a shapely silhouette behind the blinds in an upstairs window. A girl undressing for bed! I enjoyed the guilty, Peeping Tom feeling, until I realized it was Candy, in Aunt Minnie's guest room. That made it even better.

But it was time to get moving. Unplug the stupid TV and be done with it.

The loose plank in the Patellis' ancient board fence still swung open to let me through. It was a little tighter fit, but I made it — and I was in the Blitzes' yard, under the wide, ivy-covered trunk of the maple. The board steps Studs and I had nailed to the tree were still there, but I was glad to see that they had been supplemented with a ten-foot aluminum ladder.

At the top of the ladder, wedged into a low fork, was the tree house Studs and I had built in the summer of 1968. It was a triangular shed about six feet high and five feet on a side, nailed together from scrap plywood and pallet lumber. It was hard to believe it was still intact after almost thirty years. Yet, there it was.

And here I was. There were no windows, but through the cracks, I saw a blue light.

I climbed up the aluminum ladder. The door, a sheet of faux-birch paneling, was padlocked from the outside. I even recognized the padlock. Before opening it, I looked in through the wide crack at the top. I was surprised by what I saw.

Usually, when you return to scenes of your childhood, whether it's an elementary school or a neighbor's yard, everything seems impossibly small. That's what I thought it would be like with the tree house Studs and I had built when we were eleven. I expected it to look tiny inside.

Instead it looked huge.

I blinked and looked again. The inside of the tree house seemed as big as a gym. In the near corner, to the right, I saw the TV — the six-inch Dumont console. The doors were open and the gray-blue light from the screen illuminated the entire vast interior of the tree house. In the far corner, to the left, which seemed at least a half a block away, there was a brown sofa next to a potted palm.

I didn't like the looks of it. My first impulse was to climb down the ladder and go home. I even started down one step. Then I looked behind me, toward Aunt Minnie's upstairs guest room window, where I had seen Candy's silhouette. The light was out. She was in bed, waiting for me. Waiting to begin our honeymoon.

All I had to do was unplug the damn TV.

It's funny how the fingers remember what the mind forgets. The combination lock was from my old middle school locker. As soon as I started spinning the dial, my fingers knew where to start and where to stop: L-5, R-32, L-2.

I opened the lock and set it aside, hanging it on the bracket. I leaned back and pulled the door open. I guess I expected it to groan or creak in acknowledgement of the years since I had last opened it, but it made not a sound.

The last step was a long one, and I climbed into the tree house on my knees. It smelled musty, like glue and wood and old magazines. I left the door swinging open behind me. The plywood floor creaked reassuringly as I got to my feet. *Look who's back.*

The inside of the tree house looked huge, but it didn't *feel* huge. The sofa and the potted palm in the far corner seemed almost like miniatures that I could reach out and touch if I wanted to. I didn't want to. They sort of hung in the air, either real small, or real far away, or both. Or neither.

I decided it was best not to look at them. I had a job to do.

Two steps across the plywood floor took me to the corner with the TV. It was better here; more familiar. Here was the ratty rag rug my mother had donated; the Farrah Fawcett pinups on the wall. Here was the stack of old magazines: *Motor Trend*, *Boys' Life*, *Playboy*, *Model Airplane News*. Here were the ball gloves, the water guns, right where Studs and I had left them, almost thirty years before. It all looked the same, in this corner.

The TV screen was more gray than blue. There was no picture, just a steady blizzard of static and snow. The rabbit-ears antenna on the top were extended. One end was hung with tinfoil (had Studs and I done that?), and something was duct-taped into the cradle between them.

A cellular phone. I was *sure* we hadn't done that. They didn't even have cellular phones when we were kids; or duct tape, for that matter. This was clearly the other end of the connection from LaGuardia. And there was more that was new.

A green garden hose was attached to a peculiar fitting on the front of the TV, between the volume control and the channel selector. It snaked across the floor toward the corner with the brown sofa and the potted palm. The longer I looked at the hose, the longer it seemed. I decided it was best not to look at it. I had a job to do.

The electrical power in the tree house came from the house, via a "train" of extension cords winding through the branches from Studs's upstairs window. The TV was plugged into an extension cord dangling through a hole in the ceiling. I was reaching up to unplug it when I felt something cold against the back of my neck.

"Put your hands down!"

"Studs?"

"Irv, is that you?"

I turned slowly, hands still in the air.

"Irv the Perv? What the Hell are you doing here?"

"I came to unplug the television, Studs," I said. "Is that a real gun?"

"Damn tootin'," he said. "A Glock nine."

"So this is how you got all your medals!" I said scornfully. My hands still in the air, I pointed with my chin to the six-inch Dumont with the cell phone taped between the rabbit ears, then to the impressive array across Studs's chest. Even off duty, even at home, he wore his uniform with all his medals. "That's not really your Nobel Prize around your neck, either, is it?"

"It is so!" he said, fingering the heavy medallion. "The professor gave it to me. The professor helped me win the others, too, by speeding up the baggage carousel at LaGuardia. You're looking at the Employee of the Year, two years in a row."

"The professor?"

Studs pointed with the Glock nine to the other corner of the tree house. The far corner. I was surprised to see an old man, sitting on the brown sofa next to the potted palm. He was wearing a gray cardigan over blue coveralls. "Where'd he come from?" I asked.

"He comes and goes as he pleases," said Studs. "It's his Universe."

Universe? Suddenly it all came perfectly clear; or almost clear. "Dr. Radio Dgjerm?"

"Rah-dio," the old man corrected. He looked tiny but his voice sounded neither small nor far away.

"Mother took in boarders after Dad died," Studs explained. "One day I showed Dr. Dgjerm the old tree house, and when he saw the TV he got all excited. Especially when he turned it on and saw that it still worked. He bought the cell phones and set up the system."

"It doesn't really work," I said. "There's no picture."

"All those old black and white shows are off the air," said Studs. "Dr. Dgjerm had bigger things in mind than *I Love Lucy*, anyway. Like creating a new universe."

"Is that what's swelling up the inside of the tree house?" I asked.

Studs nodded. "And incidentally, helping my career." His medals clinked as his chest expanded. "You're looking at the Employee of the Year, two years in a row."

"You already told me that," I said. I looked at the old man on the sofa. "Is he real small, or far away?"

"Both," said Studs. "He's in another Universe, and it's not a very big one."

"Not big yet!" said Dr. Dgjerm. His voice sounded neither tiny nor far away. It boomed in my ear; I found out later, from Wu, that even a small universe can act as a sort of resonator or echo chamber. Like a shower.

"My Universe is small now, but it's getting bigger," Dr. Dgjerm went on. "It's a Leisure Universe, created entirely out of connective time that your Universe will never miss. In another year or so, it will attain critical mass and be big enough to survive on its own. Then I will disconnect the timelines, cast loose, and bid you all farewell!"

"We don't have another year," I said. "I have to unplug the TV now." I explained about the Butterfly Effect and the hurricanes. I even explained about my upcoming wedding in Huntsville. (I left out the part about my honeymoon, which was supposed to be going on right now, as we spoke, just three doors down and a half a floor up!)

"Congratulations," said Dgjerm in his rich Lifthatvanian accent. "But I'm afraid I can't allow you to unplug the D6. There are more than a few hurricanes and weddings at stake. We're talking about an entire new Universe, here. Shoot him, Arthur."

Studs raised the Glock nine until it was pointed directly at my face. His hand was alarmingly steady.

"I don't want to shoot you, Irv," he said apologetically. "But I owe him. He made me Employee of the Year two years in a row."

"You also took a sacred oath!" I said. "Remember? You can't shoot another Ditmas Playboy!" This wasn't just a last-ditch ploy to save my life. It was true. It was one of our bylaws; one of only two, in fact.

"That was a long time ago," said Studs, looking confused.

"Time doesn't matter to oaths," I said. (I have no idea if this is true or not. I just made it up on the spot.)

"Shoot him!" said Dr. Dgjerm.

"There's another way out of this…" said a voice behind us, "…a more civilized way."

Studs and I both turned and looked at the TV. There was a familiar (to me, at least; Studs had never met him) face in grainy black and white, wearing some sort of jungle cap.

"Wu!" I said. "Where'd you come from?"

"Real-time Internet feed," he said. "Video conferencing software. My cosmonaut friend patched me in on a rogue cable channel from a digital switching satellite. Piece of cake, once we triangulated the location through the phone signals. Although cellular video can be squirrelly. Lots of frequency bounce."

"This is a tree house? It's as big as a gymnasium!" exclaimed an oddly accented voice.

"Shut up, Dmitri. We've got a situation here. Hand me the gun, Blitz."

"You can see *out of* a TV?" I asked, amazed.

"Only a little," Wu said. "Pixel inversion piggybacked on the remote locational electron smear. It's like a reverse mortgage. Feeds on the electronic equity, so to speak, so we have to get on with it. Hand me the gun, Studs. The Glock nine."

Studs was immobile, torn between conflicting loyalties. "How can I hand a gun to a guy on TV?" he whined.

"You could set it on top of the cabinet," I suggested.

"Don't do it, Arthur!" Dr. Dgjerm broke in. "Give the gun to me. Now!"

Studs was saved. The doctor had given him an order he could obey. He tossed the Glock nine across the tree house. It got smaller and smaller and went slower and slower, until, to my surprise, Dr. Dgjerm caught it. He checked the clip and laid the gun across his tiny, or distant, or both, lap.

"We can settle this without gunplay," said Wu.

"Wilson Wu," said Dr. Dgjerm. "So we meet again!"

"Again?" I whispered, surprised. I shouldn't have been.

"I was Dr. Dgjerm's graduate assistant at Bay Ridge Realty College in the late seventies," explained Wu. "Right before he won the Nobel Prize for Real Estate."

"Which was then stolen from me!" said Dr. Dgjerm.

"The prize was later revoked by the King of Sweden," explained Wu, "when Dr. Dgjerm was indicted for trying to create an illegal Universe out of unused vacation time. Unfairly, I thought, even though technically the Time did belong to the companies."

"The charges were dropped," said Dgjerm. "But try telling that to the King of Sweden."

Studs fingered the Nobel Prize medallion. "It's not real?"

"Of course it's real!" said Dgjerm. "When you clink it, it clinks. It has mass. That's why I refused to give it back."

"Your scheme would never have worked, anyway, Dr. Dgjerm," said Wu. "I did the numbers. There's not enough unused vacation time to inflate a Universe; not anymore."

"You always were my best student, Wu," said Dgjerm. "You are right, as usual. But as you can see, I came up with a better source of Time than puny pilfered corporate vacation days." He waved his hand around at the sofa, the potted palm. "Connective Time! There's more than enough to go around. All I needed was a way to make a hole in the fabric of space-time big enough to slip it through. And I found it!"

"The D6," said Wu.

"Exactly. I had heard of the legendary Lost D6, of course, but I thought it was a myth. Imagine my surprise and delight when I found it in my own backyard, so to speak! With Arthur's help, it was a simple bandwidth problem, sluicing the connective time by phone from LaGuardia, where it would never be missed, through the D6's gauge boson rectifier twist, and into—my own Universe!"

"But it's just a sofa and a plant," I said. "Why do you want to live there?"

"Does the word 'immortality' mean anything to you?" Dgjerm asked scornfully. "It's true that my Leisure Universe is small. That's okay; the world is not yet ready for vacationing in another universe, anyway. But real estate is nothing if not a waiting game. It will get bigger. And while I am waiting, I age at a very slow rate. Life in a Universe made entirely of connective time is as close to immortality as we mortals can come."

"Brilliant," said Wu. "If you would only use your genius for science instead of gain, you could win another Nobel Prize."

"Fuck Science!" said Dgjerm, his tiny (or distant, or both) mouth twisted into a smirk as his giant voice boomed through the tree house. "I want my own universe, and I already got a Nobel Prize, so don't anybody reach for that plug. Sorry if I've thrown off your butterfly figures, Wilson, but your Universe won't miss a few more milliminutes of connective time. I will disconnect mine when it is big enough to survive and grow on its own. Not before."

"That's what I'm trying to tell you!" said Wu. "The more Universes, the better, as far as I'm concerned. Look here…"

Wu's face on the TV screen stared straight ahead, as a stream of equations flowed down over it:

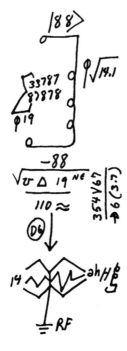

"Impossible!" said Dgjerm.

"Numbers don't lie," said Wu. "Your figures were off, professor. You reached critical mass 19.564 minutes ago, our time. Your Leisure Universe is ready to cut loose and be born. All Irv has to do is—"

"Unplug the TV?" I asked. I reached for the plug and a shot rang out.

BRANNNGGG!

It was followed by the sound of breaking glass.

CRAASH!

"You killed him!" shouted Studs.

At first I thought he meant me, but my head felt okay, and my hands were okay, one on each side of the still-connected plug. Then I saw the thick broken glass on the floor, and I knew what had happened. You know how sometimes when you fire a warning shot indoors, you hit an appliance? Well, that's what Dr. Dgjerm had done. He had meant to warn me away from the plug, and hit the television. The D6 was no more. The screen was shattered and Wu was gone.

I looked across the tree house for the sofa, the potted palm, the little man. They were flickering a little, but still there.

"You killed him!" Studs said again.

"It was an accident," said Dgjerm. "It was meant to be a warning shot."

"It was only a video conferencing image," I said. "I'm sure Wu is fine. Besides, he was right!"

"Right?" they both asked at once.

I pointed at Dr. Dgjerm. "The TV is off, and your Leisure Universe is still there."

"For now," said Dgjerm. "But the timeline is still open, and the connective time is siphoning back into your Universe." As he spoke, he was getting either smaller or farther away, or both. His voice was sounding hollower and hollower.

"What should we do?" Studs asked frantically. "Hang up the phone?"

I was way ahead of him; I had already untaped the phone and was looking for the OFF button. As soon as I pushed it, the phone rang.

It was, of course, Wu. "Everything all right?" he asked. "I lost my connection."

I told him what had happened. Meanwhile, Dr. Dgjerm was getting smaller and smaller every second. Or farther and farther away. Or both.

"You have to act fast!" Wu said. "A universe is like a balloon. You have to tie it off, or it'll shrink into nothing."

"I know," I said. "That's why I hung up the phone."

"Wrong timeline. The phone connects the baggage carousel to the D6. There must be another connection from the D6 to Dr. Dgjerm's Leisure Universe. That's the one that's still open. Look for analog, narrow bandwidth, probably green."

Dr. Dgjerm was standing on the tiny sofa, pointing frantically toward the front of the TV.

"Like a garden hose?" I asked.

"Could be," said Wu. "If so, kinking it won't help. Time

isn't like water; it's infinitely compressible. You'll have to disconnect it."

The hose was attached to a peculiar brass fitting on the front of the set, between the channel selector and the volume control. I tried unscrewing it. I turned it to the left, but nothing happened. I turned it to the right, but nothing happened. I pushed. I pulled.

Nothing happened.

"It's a special fitting!" said Dgjerm. "Special order from Chrono Supply!" I could barely hear him. He was definitely getting smaller, or farther away, or both.

"Let me try it!" said Studs, his panic showing his genuine affection for the swiftly disappearing old man. He turned the fitting to the left; he turned it to the right. He pushed, he pulled; he tugged, he twisted.

Nothing happened.

"Can I try?" asked a familiar voice.

"She can't come in here!" shouted Studs.

It was Candy, and Studs was right: NO GIRLS ALLOWED was our other bylaw. It was the bedrock of our policy. Nevertheless, ignoring his protests, I helped her off the ladder and through the door. Studs and I both gasped as she stood up, brushing off her knees. I had seen Candy out of uniform, but this was different. Very different.

She was wearing her special honeymoon lingerie from Sweet Nothings.

Nevertheless, she was all business. "It's like a childproof cap," she said. She bent down (beautifully!), and with one quick mysterious wrist-motion, disconnected the hose from the fitting. It began to flop like a snake and boom like thunder, and Candy screamed and dropped it. Meanwhile, Dr. Dgjerm was hauling the hose in and coiling it on the sofa, which was beginning to spin, slowly at first, then more and more slowly.

I heard more booming, and felt a tremendous wind sweep through the tree house.

I heard the sound of magazine pages fluttering and wood splintering.

I felt the floor tilt and I reached out for Candy as Studs yelled, "I told you so! I told you so!"

The next thing I knew, I was lying on a pile of boards under the maple tree, with Candy in my arms. Her Sweet Nothings honeymoon lingerie was short on elbow and knee protection, and she was skinned in several places. I wrapped her in my mother's old rag rug, and together we helped Studs to his feet.

"I told you so," he said.

"Told who what?"

Instead of answering, he swung at me. Luckily, he missed. Studs has never been much of a fighter. "The bylaws. NO GIRLS ALLOWED. Now look!" Studs kicked the magazines scattered around under the tree.

"It wasn't Candy!" I said. "It was your precious professor and his Leisure Universe!"

Studs swung at me again. It was easy enough to duck. A

few lights had come on in the neighboring houses, but they were already going off again. The backyard was littered with boards and magazines, ball gloves, pinups, water guns, and pocketknives. It was like the debris of childhood — it *was* the debris of childhood — all collected in one sad pile.

Studs was crying, blubbering, really, as he picked through the debris, looking (I suspected) for a little sofa, a miniature potted palm, or perhaps a tiny man knocked unconscious by a fall from a collapsing universe.

Candy and I watched for a while, then decided to help. There was no sign of Dr. Radio Dgjerm. We couldn't even find the hose. "That's a good sign," I pointed out. "The last thing I saw, he was coiling it up on the sofa."

"So?" Studs took another swing at me, and Candy and I decided it was time to leave. We were ducking down to squeeze through the loose plank in the Patellis' fence, when I heard the phone ringing behind me. It was muffled under the boards and plywood. I was about to turn back and answer it, but Candy caught my arm — and my eye.

It was still our honeymoon, after all, even though I had a headache from the fall. So, I found out later, did Candy.

I thought that was the end of the Ditmas Playboys, but the next day at LaGuardia, Studs was waiting for us at the top of the escalator to Gates 1–17. He had either cleaned or changed his uniform since the disaster of the night before, and his medals gleamed, though I noticed he had taken off the Nobel Prize.

At first I thought he was going to take a swing at me, but instead he took my hand.

"Your friend Wu called last night," he said. "Right after you and what's-her-name left."

"Candy," I said. "My fiancée." She and Aunt Minnie were standing right beside me, but Studs wouldn't look at them. Studs had always had a hard time with girls and grown-ups — which is why I was surprised that he had become so attached to Dr. Dgjerm. Perhaps it was because the brilliant but erratic Lifthatvanian realtor was, or seemed, so small, or far away, or both.

"Whatever," said Studs. "Anyway, your friend told me that, as far as he could tell, the Leisure Universe was cast loose and set off safely. That Dr. Dgjerm survived."

"Congratulations," I said. "Now if you'll excuse me, we have a plane to catch."

"What a nice boy that Arthur is," said Aunt Minnie, as we boarded the plane. I felt no need to respond, since she was talking to Uncle Mort and not to me. "And you should see all those medals!"

The departure was late. I found that oddly reassuring. Candy sat in the middle, her eyes tightly closed, and I let Aunt Minnie have the window seat. It was her first flight. She pressed the urn with Uncle Mort's ashes to the window for the takeoff.

"It's his first flight," she said. "I read in *Reader's Digest* that you're less nervous when you can see what's going on."

"I don't believe it," muttered Candy, her eyes closed tightly.

"And how can ashes be nervous, anyway?"

The planes may be old on PreOwned Air, but the interiors have been refurbished several times. They even have the little credit card phones on the backs of the seats. There was nobody I wanted to talk to for fifteen dollars a minute, but I wasn't surprised when my phone rang.

"It's me. Did the plane leave late?"

"Eighteen minutes," I said, checking my notes.

"Numbers don't lie!" said Wu. "Things are back to normal. I already knew it, in fact, because my calculations came out perfect this morning. I released the first moth in the rain forest at 9:14 A.M., Eastern Standard Time."

I heard a roar behind him, which I assumed was rain.

"Congratulations," I said. "What about Dr. Dgjerm and his Leisure Universe?"

"It looks like the old man made it okay," said Wu. "If his Universe had crashed, my figures wouldn't have come out so good. Of course, we will never know for sure. Now that our Universe and his are separated, there can be no exchange of information between them. Not even light."

"Doesn't sound like a good bet for a resort," I said.

"Dgjerm didn't think it all the way through," said Wu. "This was always his weakness as a realtor. However, he will live forever, or almost forever, and that was important to him also. Your friend Studs cried with relief, or sadness, or both when I told him last night. He seems very attached to the old man."

"He's not exactly a friend," I said. "More like a childhood

acquaintance."

"Whatever," said Wu. "How was your Honeymoon?"

I told him about the headache(s). Wu and I have no secrets. I had to whisper, since I didn't want to upset Candy. She might have been asleep, but there was no way to tell; her eyes had been closed since we had started down the runway.

"Well, you can always try again after the ceremony," Wu commiserated.

"I intend to," I said. "Just make sure you get to Huntsville on time with the ring!"

"It'll be tight, Irv. I'm calling from a trimotor just leaving Quetzalcan City."

"An L1011? A DC-10?" The roar sounded louder than ever.

"A Ford Trimotor," Wu said. "I missed the nonstop, and it's a charter, the only thing I could get. It'll be tight. We can only make 105 mph."

"They stopped making Ford Trimotors in 1929. How can they have cell phones?"

"I'm in the cockpit, on the radio. The pilot, Huan Juan, and I went to flight school together in Mukden."

Why was I not surprised? I leaned over to look out the window, and saw the familiar runways of Squirrel Ridge, the airport, far below.

"We're getting ready to land," I said. "I'll see you at the wedding!"

I hung up the phone. Aunt Minnie held the urn up to the window. Candy shut her eyes even tighter.

*

Divorces are all alike, according to Dostoyevsky, or some Russian, but marriages are each unique, or different, or something. Our wedding was no exception.

It started off great. There's nothing like a morning ceremony. My only regret was that Candy couldn't get the whole day off.

The weather was perfect. The sun shone down from a cloudless sky on the long, level lawn of the Squirrel Ridge Holiness Church. Cindy's catering van arrived at ten, and she and the two kids, Ess and Em, started unloading folding tables and paper plates, plastic toothpicks and cut flowers, and coolers filled with crab cakes and ham biscuits for the open-air lunchtime reception.

All Candy's friends from the Huntsville Parks Department were there, plus the friends we had in common, like Bonnie from the Bonny Baguette (who brought her little blackboard; it was like her brain) and Buzzer from Squirrel Ridge, the nursing home, complete with diamond stud nose ring. My friend Hoppy from the Hoppy's Good Gulf, who happened to be a Holiness preacher, was officiating. (" 'Course I'll marry Whipper Will's young-un to Whipper Will's Yank. 'Nuff said.")

Aunt Minnie looked lovely in her colorful Lifthatvanian peasant costume (red and blue, with pink lace around the sleeves) smelling faintly of mothballs. Even Uncle Mort sported a gay ribbon 'round his urn.

It was all perfect, except—where was Wu?

"He'll be here," said Cindy as she unpacked the ice sculpture of Robert E. Lee's horse, Traveller (the only thing the local ice sculptor knew how to do), and sent Ess and Em to arrange the flowers near the altar.

"He's on a very slow plane," I said.

Finally, we felt like we had to get started, best man or no. It was 11:55 and the guests were beginning to wilt. I gave a reluctant nod and the twin fiddles struck up "The Wedding March"—

And here came the bride. I hadn't seen Candy since the night before. She looked resplendent in her dress-white uniform, complete with veil, her medals gleaming in the sun. Her bridesmaids all wore khaki and pink.

Since I was short a ring, Hoppy slipped me the rubber o-ring from the front pump of a Ford C-6 transmission. "Use this, Yank," he whispered. "You can replace it with the real one later."

"Brethren and sistren and such, we are gathered here today..." Hoppy began. Then he stopped, and cocked his head toward a distant buzzing sound. "Is that a Ford?"

It was indeed. There is nothing that stops a wedding like a "Tin Goose" setting down on a church lawn. Those fat-winged little airliners can land almost anywhere.

This one taxied up between the ham biscuit and punch tables, and shut down all three engines with a couple of backfires and a loud *cough-cough*. The silence was deafening.

The little cabin door opened, and out stepped a six-foot Chinaman in a powder-blue tux and a scuffed leather helmet. It was my best man, Wilson Wu. He took off the helmet as he jogged up the aisle to polite applause.

"Sorry I'm late!" he whispered, slipping me the ring.

"What's with the blue tux?" I knew it wasn't the one I had reserved for him at Five Points Formal Wear.

"Picked it up last night during a fuel stop in Bozeman," he said. "It was prom night there, and blue was all they had left."

Hoppy was pulling my sleeve, asking me questions. "Of course I do!" I said. "You bet I do!" There was the business with the ring, the real one. ("Is that platinum or just white gold?" Cindy gasped.) Then it was time to kiss the bride.

Then it was time to kiss the bride again.

As soon as the ceremony was over, the twin fiddles struck up "Brand-New Tennessee Waltz," and we all drifted back to the tables in the shade of the Trimotor for refreshments. We found an unfamiliar Mayan-Chinese-looking dude eyeing the shrimp, and made him welcome. It was Wu's pilot friend, Huan Juan. Ess and Em served the congealed salad, after shrieking and hugging their father whom they hadn't seen in six weeks.

"I should have known better than to worry, Wu," I said. "But did you say Bozeman? I thought that was in Montana."

"It is," he said, filling his plate with potato salad. "It's not on the way from eastern Quetzalcan to northern Alabama, unless you take the Great Triangle Route."

I knew he wanted me to ask, so I did: "The what?"

Smiling proudly, Wu took a stack of ham biscuits. "You

know how a Great Circle Route looks longer on a map, but is in fact the shortest way across the real surface of the spherical Earth?"

"Uh huh." I grabbed some more of the shrimp. They were going fast. The twin fiddles launched into "Orange Blossom Special."

"Well, a triangle is the shortest route across the negatively folded surface of space-time. Look."

Wu took what I thought was a map out of the pocket of his tux and unrolled it. It was covered with figures:

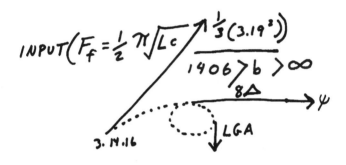

"As you can see, it's sort of counterintuitive," he said. "It means flying certain strict patterns and altitudes, and, of course, it only works in a three-engine plane. But there it is. The shortest Great Triangle Space-Time Route from Quetzalcan City to Huntsville traverses the high plains and skims the edge of Chesapeake Bay."

"Amazing," I said. The shrimp, which are as big as pistol grips, are grown in freshwater ponds in western Kentucky. I couldn't stop eating them.

"Numbers don't lie," said Wu. "Not counting fuel stops — and with a Ford Trimotor there are lots of those — it took Huan Juan and me only twenty-two hours to fly 6476.54 miles in a plane with a top speed of one hundred and twelve mph. Let me try one of those giant shrimp."

"That's great," I said, looking through the thinning crowd for Candy. "But it's almost 12:20, and Candy has to be at work at one."

Wu looked shocked. "No honeymoon?"

I shook my head. "Candy traded shifts for the trip to New York, and now she has to work nights, plus all weekend."

"It's not very romantic," said Candy, edging up beside me. "But it was the best we could do. Huan Juan, have you tried the giant shrimp?"

The pilot nodded without answering. He and Wu were consulting in whispers. They looked up at the clear blue sky, then down at the calculations on the unrolled paper.

"They are intimately entwined," I heard Wu say (I thought he was talking about Candy and me; I found out later he was talking about Time and Space). "All you have to do to unravel and reverse them is substitute this N for this 34.8, and hold steady at 2622 feet and ninety-seven mph, air speed. Can you fly it?"

Huan Juan nodded, reaching for another giant shrimp.

"What's going on?" I asked.

"Let's take a ride," said Wu, snapping his leather helmet under his chin. "Don't look so surprised. This Trimotor's equipped with a luxury Pullman cabin; it once belonged to a Latin American dictator."

"Where are we going?" I asked, pulling Candy to my side.

"Nowhere! We are going to fly a Great Triangle configuration, compressed and reversed, over Squirrel Ridge for twenty-three minutes, and you will experience it as, let's see — " he squinted, figuring, "—two point six hours of honeymoon time. Better bring along some giant shrimp and ham biscuits."

Cindy handed Candy a bouquet. Hoppy and Bonnie and all our friends were applauding.

"What about—you know?" I whispered to Candy. I meant the honeymoon lingerie she had bought at Sweet Nothings.

With a shy smile she pulled me aside. While Em and Ess tied shoes to the tail of the plane, and while Huan Juan and Wu cranked up the three ancient air-cooled radials with a deafening roar, and while the rest of the guests polished off the giant shrimp, Candy opened the top button of her tunic to give me a glimpse of what she was wearing underneath.

Then we got on the plane and soared off into the wild blue. And that's another story altogether.

Author's Afterword

THESE THREE TALES of Wilson Wu and his "Watson," Irving, were originally published in *Asimov's*. One of them even got a Hugo nomination. But I was not happy. It was always my dream to gather them together into one little novel. I felt they belonged together.

Bob Kruger's ElectricStory did them up beautifully as an e-book. Then they appeared in France, from Gallimard, as *Échecs et Maths*. But still I mourned. Until now.

It might interest the reader to know that *Numbers Don't Lie* is based on real events.

My friend Pat Molloy, an aerospace insider, slipped me the specs on the lunar rover.

Rudy Rucker checked out all of Wu's math formulae for both accuracy and elegance. He assures me that the one is more important the other.

The Hole in Brooklyn is a real place, as is (or was) Frankie's junkyard of Volvos.

The Nobel Prize for Real Estate has been discontinued.

As for the kerosene-powered fax machine and the ice sculpture of Robert E. Lee's horse, Traveller — *où sont les neiges d'antan?*